Me the Old Man

also by Bill Reed
novels (*available in printed-book and ebook formats*)
Dogod
The Pipwink Papers\
Me, the Old Man
Stigmata
Ihe
Crooks
Tusk
Throw her back
Are You Human?
Awash
1001 Lankan Nights book 1
1001 Lankan Nights book 2

Nonfiction
Water Workout

professionally-staged/ published plays
Burke's Company*
Truganinni*
The Pecking Order
Mr Siggie Morrison with his Comb and Paper*
The Old Pig Rat
Jack Charles is Up and Fighting
Just Out of Your Ground
You Want It, Don't You, Billy?
I Don't Know What to Do with You*.
Paddlesteamer
Cass Butcher Bunting*
Bullsh
More Bullsh
Talking to a Mirror*
Auntie and the Girl*
*Available in print and ebook formats

award-winning short stories *(see title 'Passing Strange')*
Messman on the C.E. Altar
English Expression
The 200-year Old Feet
The Case Inside
Blind Freddie Among the Pickle Jars
The Old Ex-serviceman
Mahood on the Thin Beach
The Shades of You my Dandenong

BILL REED
with Edward Nugent

a novel

First published in 1979 by Rigby
This reprint published independently by Reed Independent 2015
Melbourne, Australia
reedindependent@gmail.com

Printed by CreateSpace, an Amazon.com company

Available from Amazon.com, CreateSpace.com, and other retail outlets. Ebook
formats are available from all major online ebook retailers.
paperback: ISBN13-9780994280503
ebook: ISBN13-9780994239945

Cover re-creation: Lahiru Sameera, Dart Lanka Production, Colombo, Sri Lanka

National Library of Australia Cataloguing-in-Publication entry:
(paperback)
Author: Reed, Bill, 1939 -   author.
Title: Me, the Old Man / Bill Reed
ISBN: 9780994280503
Subjects: Australia—Fiction/social violence/tragic-comic
Dewey Number: A823.3

(ebook)
Author: Reed, Bill, 1939 -   author.
Title: Me, the Old Man/ Bill Reed
ISBN: 9780994239945
Subjects: Australia—Fiction/social violence/tragic-comic
Dewey Number: A823.3

MANTISSAE

A.

This is true: In 1965, a sixty-five-year-old man became trapped down a storm drain in a park in Sydney. He was caught under debris and immersed in water for up to three weeks or more. Children discovered him early on, but they did not tell their parents. They fed him a few scraps and lowered down a small bottle of water each day. When the debris was lifted from the old man's legs, it was found that they had gangrened. The men who lifted the debris vomited on the spot.

B.

This is also true: There is Edward Nugent, parts of whose writings I have used here to form the consciousness of the old man in the storm drain. Edward is seventy-nine years old. He lives in a not unpleasant tiny room in the Salvation Army hostel in Linden Park, Adelaide. I have not altered the spelling, the style or the expressions of his writings.

1.

The old man is thinking while I write this. You might soon know where he is as he is thinking while I write this...

Helopolis, Egypt. Started of with brand new Wellington. After test was...

but the old man will not know where he is thinking, what his surroundings are, most of the time. He knows he is trapped down a storm drain, or does he? He knows he is in his little one-room council flat back in Belfast, or does he? He knows he is in his killing little private hotel room back in Sydney slowly going killed, or does he? He knows he is back in the dank cellar in a suburb he's forgotten the name of and a city he hasn't thought of for years, where some welfare people discovered him and rescued him (that was years ago), or does he?

It doesn't matter, for the old man is thinking while I write this.

... new Wellington. After test was declared O.K. Loaded with fuel. Ammo for Malta. Lovely morning. Give pilot course. Got to Malta. They had to shove some Spits out of the way so we could land. Malta was in a hell of a state, Plastered by jerries, night and

2.

One.

Item. 'The spirit of independence', the Belfast paper declared one day in December 1978 (I have changed the date), 'so often found among old people is remarkable. The Belfast Society for the Elderly has reported that, after a long wait of many years, an elderly Irish/ Australian was at last fixed up with an assisted passage back to his adopted homeland. It was tactfully suggested that new shirts might be provided for the journey, but the old man thought nothing of this and said he intended to travel in his best white silk shirt which he had purchased in Australia for the first of his trips back to this, his original birthplace — 45 years ago!'

Two.

When the old man left Belfast this time to come back 'home' once and for all, it was right that he should make a little puff of news. It wasn't only that he had been forty- five years trying to get back to Australia. It wasn't that, for the last six years, he had 'lay' outside the Australian Migration Office in Belfast and there silently pleaded with his large brown eyes for the rules to be bent so that he could get an assisted passage home. It was rather that the old man had become such a little pet-thing of so many people. Not of ridicule. Not of protectiveness. (Only the Commissioner Mogg of the newspaper office would give him the bum's-rush if he sat in there too long reading the free paper on a cold afternoon.) But as everyone's marionette.

One or other of his 'dear friends' had given him most of everything he owned. The rest of his 'things' came from the Elderly Society — or through a quick jerk of compassion by one of the local government agencies. His little flat in Belfast's inner ring, for example... the one he was leaving behind to return to Australia... with its wall-to-wall carpet and the bright colours on the wall and the all-night heater that switched itself on, *protecting,* council-provided and 'dear friend' furnished, gratis gratis.

The old man even spoke marionette. His little voice modulating with his little large brown eyes watching for effect nonetheless closely for being sidelong, both it and his eyes. And tiny. Five four in his socks, he would say. But always exaggerating a little. Pixy or marionette? Shrewd or manipulated? No matter; whichever way, for someone on the make he had that one saving grace that everything about him was little. Little and sweet. We all know how it goes. Women loved him just to look at him and thought of cots.

He shuffled along with eager little jerks. As though his little legs wanted to break into a little trot but he couldn't manage it. And of course he had his little routine for the day. Trippingly going on his little round with a little flower or a little apple or a little banana or a little story for whoever was his self-appointed protector in, say, the newspaper office, the Chinese restaurant, the migration office, the local library, the butcher shop, the bakery, the donation office of the Elderly Society. And that, generally without variance, was his daily routine. In Belfast. Before he got his assisted passage back 'home'. That routine generally ending back at the newspaper office in time for the first evening edition.

It must be avowed here that the old man's little gifts were received by his 'dear friends' with shrieks of delight and back-of-hand giggles... sleight? Isn't he a little living doll? But then, again, seen as little shares in a greater investment, givings-to-get-given, who cares anyway? I am writing fictionally.

Three.

So the old man finally managed to persuade them to give him an assisted passage back to Australia, his adopted 'home', after forty-five years. He unpacked the shirt he had bought in Australia those forty-five years ago. They don't make them like this nowadays etcetera etcetera. He arrived an hour early at the Belfast bus terminus that connected with the airport, in case Fate contrived an anachronology on every time piece in the city.

The old man wanted to get on every bus and every plane, in case the case was that if he missed the first one of either he would surely miss the one he was supposed to catch. He also took his own tomato sandwiches in case. In case of what? In case. He had twenty-five well-wishers to see him off, all but one women. Nobody knew who the man was, not even the old man. Say it was me. He posted a letter back to a Mrs Holland during the stop-over at Singapore. He wrote ten lines to her. He said that the hostesses had been lovely and kind, but he thought one of them deliberately went around tempting men but he would have to find out more about this before writing again, and he was writing from Singapore.

He had arrived 'home', soon after, at last. After forty-five years. He had written before leaving his council flat back in Belfast to his only living relatives. They lived in Sydney, he thought. They would be delighted to hear the glad news, he thought. They were his married sister living in Gosford and his single younger brother living care of somewhere.

Four.
The old man was 'home'. He had all the nasty little bugs sprayed off him at Kingsford Smith Airport. Yes, 'home'. To what?

Five.

He could not find his brother. No sister was there to meet him at the airport. His brother had 'gone off somewhere'. His sister was out when he knocked at the door. The old man's brother-in-law was in. His sister's house was full as it was, he said. She had got his letter, sure pal, but she thought he'd know that his sister's house was full already, for Christ's sake. The old man heard rustling of someone from inside the house, behind the door. Was it his sister? Did he think that? He can't remember now. He is a bit tired now, *wafting*. Perhaps his sister had been ill. The old man would never know. Did he hear the rustling of his sister for the last time then? His brother-in-law didn't invite him in. But he did say the old man could leave where he was staying and his sister would write to him when she got back in 'a few days'.

But the old man was staying in a cheap private hotel in town and he couldn't afford to stay another night in that hotel, so he couldn't leave his sister an address so that she could write and tell him how delighted she was to hear that he had arrived back home. *Home.* So she could tell him how sorry she was that their house was already full. So she could tell him dear me it wasn't me that was rustling behind the door.

They would not give him his pension, right off. It takes time to arrange a pension. The pension scheme between Northern Ireland and Australia is a bit more complicated than just walking in here and asking for your weekly pension, excuse me.

But the welfare people here are just as slowly kind as they are over in Belfast and he managed to kip down in another private hotel in Redfem. We should read hovel for hotel there... is that the old man's thought now or am I writing it? The landlord didn't like the little poofta's looks and his wife would have been chewing betel nut in Borneo had she been bom there. She had never dreamt of cots and had never believed in penniless pixies or moneyless marionettes or poor old men. Dirty old Irish buggers. And

he never ever found out where his brother had moved to because his never-sister never did write care of. And he never did write to her again or go out to Gosford to worry her again. And he fell down the slip-sure-as steps in that private hotel one day and chipped a bone in his little old ankle and it didn't help that he was just beginning to suffer a little Parkinson's Disease although he was never to know it and the landlord cursingly took him around the comer to the hospital. Where he left the old man in the car park and drove off. Well, what else was he supposed to do?

Where the old man waited alone in pain for two hours in the Outpatient's Department. Experienced some bonhomie and cheer during his two weeks in the ward, where there were a few nurses who had not seen it all, until they presented him with the bill. No, a Northern Ireland/Britain National Health Number is not transferrable to Australia, whaddyathink it is. This is the land of private enterprise, that totem carried by only the inner members of the tribe.

But the welfare people helped some there again. Finally they managed to get his pension through, too. And when he returned to his private hovel, he crept up the stairs to find his room locked against him and when he came back downstairs he saw that his suitcase had been placed out on the landing outside the landlord's room with the door firmly shut. It had not been out on that landing when he had hobbled up the stairs to his old room.

They had slit two knife-cuts in the cardboard suitcase he now used, but had found there was nothing in there that could

9

compensate them for the sudden loss of two day's rent before they found someone else for the room.

He tried his brother's old address for the very last time. There was no word. They still did not know where the brother had gone to live. They never heard of the brother. That was so long ago. They could not remember if the brother ever got a letter from Belfast. They could not remember seeing the brother post a reply back to the old man because they'd never heard of the brother. There was no word. The old man never found his only brother, his younger brother. If he was thinking this now, he would not even know if his younger brother was alive today. I am writing that the old man would sorely wish that.

And all the smiles and pert little pouts and all his seekings-out of the Nightingale women who he thought lurked somewhere in every situation and institution... these did nothing. Absolutely. Sydney is of sterner stuff than Belfast. There are no dwellings at the bottom of the gardens in Sydney for small folk. Fairies are force-fed down at the local cop stations. And where once his clothes had shone with lookee-me, now there were greys of cast-off, old-age- age-old dull gabardines. No sparkle anymore. Nor in his little large brown eyes. Only the smell of his body and every room in which he was welcome for a while underpinned by that brown over-worn lino and the unknown coughings from the rows of beds around, over and under him.

Six.

The sun rarely shone that summer, his first back 'home'. That autumn. Coming on winter, the sun rarely shone. Only the parchnesses and the grey-graded shadows of the tormented gums. In forty-five years, the gums had lost their glory. They weren't somehow the ones he had spoken about to his 'dear friends' in Belfast all those long months ago. In forty-five years, all the grass had been burnt browner. The flowers never seemed to open much anymore. No substance in the thin grassy cushions for the thin leather under his little old flat aching feet, seemingly.

For the first time in his life, he had begun to shiver. The old man's bones began to make themselves felt and arctic and ageing. Jarring on asphalt. Such a hard trudge to the nearest park. Where the colour green is. Of Belfast. Of Northern Ireland. Of Eire the Whole. You can't park here.

The sun seemed rarely to shine and for the first time in his life the old man felt cold. The dark and secret folds of closed-off people back at 'home'.

The old man wrote back to his friends in Belfast and told them he was unhappy. He wrote back to them and told them he had no money. He had no friends left at 'home'. This wasn't his home. The old man wrote he realised that this was not his home after all. He could not find his brother. His sister's house was full already. He had broken his ankle and had been thrown out of his room and where he lived now, it was a sort of dormitory. The sun didn't seem to shine as much as it used to when he was last 'home', he wrote. Now it was autumn and the sun hadn't shone much at all all through spring and summer, he wrote.

And he wrote to his friends back in Belfast saying how much he missed them.

And, when they read his letters, they laughed sadly and were still mentioning the letters solemnly, shaking their heads, for years after. But not too much. For the conversations only. After all, the old man had gone 'home' even though they had tried to warn him about old age and the senility of tricks in olden minds. But, still, they laughed sadly for him because in his letters he had begun to hint that, if someone would lend him the return fare back to his little council flat in Belfast, he would pay them back somehow. They knew him, you know me. If someone would do that he would like to

return to Belfast return to his friends return to his little council flat return to where he had lived for forty-five years return to where his mother had been bom and his father had been bom and return to where he knew he really belonged now and return to where people thought where they weren't so ignorant of thinking as these Australians where to think wasn't to be a little poof where there were thoughts, yes.

Seven.
The old man had been back 'home' in Australia a full six months. Six months ago, the forty-five-year-old dream had begun to end.

Eight.
One day the old man pulled out his cardboard suitcase from under that unknown dormitory's unknown bed. He put on his little white silk shirt that had been the subject of that newspaper article, the shirt which he had bought in Australia forty-five years ago. He put on the blowy corduroy trousers he used to wear as best in Belfast. His little large brown eyes were red. His little large brown eyes were red and his little old bones were aching and there was a buzzing in his head. He seemed not to hear all those other old men in that dormitory laugh at him as he walked out. He walked out of that building. He seemed not to hear the matron, that blowsed whale of that place, calling sharply to him. He walked. The old man walked.

He seemed not to hear or see the one or two nudges 'get a load

12

of that', sometimes even sympathetic among themselves, from the healthy inner-tribe Australian workers on this place or that place as he walked by. Little steps. He walked as far as he could, did the old man. A long way, yes. Little marionette. Until he made it to the park. That great open green park of Sydney that he knew of from all those memories ago. On the way he only stopped once.

Nine.
He only stopped once. It was in the middle of a Sydney intersection. The old man stopped suddenly, stopping the through traffic, jolted up, as though all his little strings had been scissored. Stock still, then. And someone — was it me or is he merely thinking that someone might have — heard him say in a tone of simple fact that he had never quite used before:

'What am I doing here?'

Then simply walked on until he reached his park. The park whose name he most remembered. A huge, open parkland. There are storm drains in there. He took off his little shoes. He held his little shoes in his little old left hand and held his other palm, little and pink and old, high above his little right arm and he walked right on in.

His little old cardboard suitcase stood on the path behind him.

Ten.
18 June 1979. The date is my date. The morning after one of the children had told his father and the old man was found, the newspaper reports were more varied than extensive. There wasn't very much at all about the old man. Only the editorial, which was a bit of a fluke, really, otherwise I might never have heard about the old man and might not have been writing

13

right now and laying myself out to the charge of usingd him..

On that day, after all, there had been plenty of newsworthy competition. Another near-old man was burnt to death with kero while waiting for a bus, thrown on him by passing ha-ha youths, and then the match. Somewhere else a ritual hanging with spun threads of piano wire; the child hanging there was seven years old and female. No, our old man was hardly even newsworthy enough for the daily moral lesson hereby giveth. Nevertheless, it must have been newsworthy enough — or am I just writing that it was, or is the old man just thinking now that he would be newsworthy enough but is only daydreaming? Page four, the editorial page; you might remember:

MAN STARVES, ROTS IN DRAIN.
Children tell tale of stunning cruelty.
An 11-year-old boy yesterday led police to the shocking remains of an elderly man who had apparently been trapped down a storm drain in Racecourse Park. The man was wedged under iron sheeting and was lying in a few feet of water. The old man's flesh had rotted below the waist. The boy told police that he and two other children had known the old man had been trapped down there and had brought him a biscuit and a bottle of water each day. He had apparently been down there well over a fortnight. No reasons have been given yet as to why they did not even tell their parents of the old man's plight. A police spokesman surmised that the old man, whose name has not been released, must have gone to sleep down the storm drain and then got trapped under iron sheeting during the flash floods of a few weeks ago. The actual cause of the death has yet to be ascertained. Heart attack, starvation, exposure and gangrene are some of the causes being investigated by the police.'

14

Obviously, it was not the editorial. I don't know why I wrote that it was. Perhaps the old man was thinking that he might make the editorial. Perhaps he ought to have. But he did get that item on the editorial page, tucked away. And there was in the editorial itself a ten-line paragraph that commented adversely on the nation's moral fibre when even children so young can callously let an old man starve and/or rot to death.

Eleven.
They recovered the little old man's little brown hat from the nine-year-old boy's room. He was the younger of the two boys; the third child was the girl. But the old man's sister did not want the police or the one reporter to come into the house and the brother still could not be traced. Besides, the old man has forgotten them already.

Twelve.
Novel. Novella. Nonnovel notnovella. Novellanovel. Some of this is fiction. I don't know anymore how much of this is fiction, or how much is fact. Am I writing this as a statement of how I am writing this — that is, how it is *turning out* (what is this: a lathe?)? Or is this the old man thinking that he doesn't know how much he is thinking is real and how much isn't real. Am I using the old man; is the old man using me?

He does not know how he will or will not be part of my fiction as he lies down there as he once did, dying. I don't know how much I am imagining all this, or how much I am only a part of his imagination — how he wants what he is finally thinking down there in that storm drain to be written about and put, finally so that all am see, into a book. A book; a fact; suck that and see; take that away. A book is a life. Is he fulfilled by this book or am I using what I know to be a universal egocentricity in all men to get at the old man's thought and put my own name on a book? Whose fiction is this?

But the old man is down the storm drain. I write about the old man being down the storm drain and the old man thinks about him being down there. Oh, either way, he *is*. Either way you look at it the old man is down the storm drain... as he ever was, or ever has been, down the storm drain. Novel. Novella. He is our fiction as ever as much as he was our fact, too. And likewise.

Does it matter? As long as the old man's voice bursts through. As long as someone says, 'The old man is thinking' about the old man thinking. They say your humanedness will burst through. The old man says, 'But this is my face; don't I shine through anymore?' His voice breaking through. He died without a whimper, without the laying on of ears on him, or did he, or didn't he? That is why his voice keeps breaking through here. It is the fiction.

3.

He, the old man, has lain in dank for how many days until now? He hasn't bothered to keep count. He might have tried, though, and lost count. But I would have thought he wouldn't have kept count because he would have thought it ridiculous if you told him he wasn't going to be rescued around the next minute. Let's leave it at that.

The old man has stopped yelling, for nobody comes. Only the children. They come when they want, not when the old man yells as loud as he can. Which isn't too loud. He doesn't feel much like yelling anymore anyway. He has given up trying to heave off the weight that pins down his little old legs in the silt and filth of the sludge in the water in the storm drain in the parkland somewhere in the heart of Sydney. He only

looks up now at the hole through which he had fallen. His neck aches. But he tries to keep looking upwards. No longer calls out in hope for rescue; he has given up shouting. Just watching for a break in the clouds so vertically up there. He is thinking; I told you he was thinking.

It must not be forgotten that thought is the master of thinking. You see something that interests but you haven't time just then to attend to it but the thought is implanted in your mind. Make every thought a captive. If you have a thought like mine that thought will come up sooner or later. As I write this I am listening to Emperor Concerto, Beethoven. I've got lots of beautiful music (cassette). No man is lonely with good music and books. You will have thoughts come into your head that seem to have at that time nothing to do with what you are doing, ie, a word kept coming into my head that had nothing to do with what I was doing. This bothered me a bit. I hate being at a

17

loss about anything. The word was KANSA. This is Arabic for number 5. On occasions I go to the Sportsman Hotel. There were pictures of Dickins characters hung on the walls, now another name bothered me. Suddenly the name came to me 'Quilp'. Anyone who has ever read Dickins, Charles, will know who Quilp was. Quilp finished up in Australia.

But the clouds above the old man do not break. Sometimes they thinned. Sometimes they stretched themselves out in long strands. But mostly they thicken and get a little lighter and then thicken again. It rained. If it rains heavy again, like in the first two nights he was down there, he will be able to hear the water first before it starts gushing down the drain. Today was the drier.

Not for the first time he begins to smell himself. At first he didn't know what it was, except that it is quite pleasant. It wasn't strong at first. It was frank and delicate. When he realised that it was his own body rotting, but didn't know it was rotting, he eased a bit of the debris aside so that the smell came at him. He sucked in great draughts of it. It didn't put him off at all. It was comforting. And the old man is remembering that he should not forget those he has sought to think stink.

There was a jew millionaire in Germany named Sharlaz. How he escaped the concentration camps I'll never know. He organised his own small army. He directed them to shoot as many Germans as possible. You will note I said 'directed'. He hadn't the guts to do any shooting himself. I don't know what happened to him but I hope someone shot him.

In Belfast, Northern Ireland

before the council flat before his friends before the Society for the Elderly and his little daily routine before he had developed his own way of surviving and make-living. He had got too old to work anymore and found that he had not much to live on after all; no one friend after all; working all your life wasn't enough after all. Nobody wanted to listen to an Irish-Australian. Alone, then. Before the little marionette routine got worked out. Alone, trying to crab at life on his own terms. Alone and now living in a Belfast cellar in a mostly-deserted Belfast slum terrace.

He was sixty and it seemed that his little old life had already come to an end.

The cellar, in which he lay alone in Belfast, stank like a storm drain. He is still thinking of those people he was told have always stank, the root causes.

> On being invalided out of the R.A.F. in 1942, I rented a bombed-out shop. The agent was Cayser. Another jew. I fixed it up and tried to sell hardware but this was a dead loss. I applied to food office for permit to sell food stuffs. The food office said, get 25 people to sign that they will buy from you and we will give you a licence. I not only got licence but cigarette people supplied me with cigarette rations. Needless to say this jew went mad and threatened to throw me out. I said get stuffed and try it. He couldn't. Another jew. I had a loan from him. Can't remember his name. He took out a summons against me but he forgot to state that I had done plumbing work for him to pay debt but he didn't state this in court and magistrate threw him out of court with some scathing remarks.

When the wreckers came to pull down the terrace, they were surprised to find anyone living there. They were surprised to find the old man living in that Belfast cellar. The rat exterminator who was there as an observer reported in to the Belfast Council about him. At the council chambers, they dispatched a catholic female welfare officer to the old man. She arrived and saw how he was living; she took him over. She was the wrong religion but he didn't care. He hadn't had much to do with women before. Not in this way.

He began to discover. He began his discovery of the frustrated mother of marionettes in them all.

He continues in the living comforts of the council flat she got for him and his new 'dear friends' are furnishing. Who is going to tell him he is not there, but storm-drained? Not her anymore.

> I have promised to write a book for one of my ladies here and although she may have been sylpth like once she is well upholstered now so I have to use a fair amount of imagination now. She once attended ballet so I will have to try to imagine her in ballet now which is going to be tough going.

> Thoughts. The thought is captive. There is no doubt about it I make things tough for myself. This typewriter I am using now, I had to save up the money for it and do my own typing and if one has not handled a typewriter before this is hard work and publishers don't help you much. But I'm a glutten for punishment so I'll manage somehow or other.

When the children came back to the storm drain, they laughed down at him. After the first three days, he stopped asking them to help him. They came to know his sign language for food and drink. The first time they gave him a biscuit, they lowered it down on a piece of string. He pulled on it desperately as though it was a life-line. But they let it go their end. It was only an old bit of string anyway so they wouldn't get into trouble about losing it. They only laughed down at the old man.

Now he coughs. Something inside of him is on fire. He feels his little old heart flutter. He begins to feel something in him saying that it is Parkinson's disease, but he doesn't know what it is saying. But he continues to watch the sky. But grey and flatly patched. But it must be getting on late afternoon. After school time and the children again. Another day when the sun hasn't strobed a single ray down on him. Where are you, where is he?

A clean comfortable bed. Good food. I have a clean comfortable room, they don't bother me and I hope I don't bother them. After being washed around by the waves of two wars I have been washed up on this beach and it's a hell of a lot more comfortable than some other beaches I've known. Example, I have never yet asked for help and been refused. If anything goes wrong it's my own fault. I have friends and very helpful they are, I must mention a few names here. Polly, kitchen staff, it doesn't matter what I want she will get it for me. A friend in need is a friend indeed. And Dossie who does the cleaning. To lift my arms and make my own bed causes me a lot of needless pain. And then there is Rayleen, Falls Rd Library, who gets me all the intellectual books I need. I have no need to ask for any particular books, I leave it to the excellent taste of Rayleen. The trouble is I am getting into a routine, this I don't like as routine disables thought. You will no doubt wonder what the hell a man nearly eighty requires intellectual books for. Well, I've always been that way inclined. To sit still without thinking would

21

be impossible for me, perhaps I am suffering from an organic disease of the brain, but things that interest me I want to know all about and the things I want to know about are almost innumerable. Rayleen brought me a book by Robert Ardrey (African Genesis). This is one of the best books I have ever read.

The old man lets his head fall back. It doesn't matter where he puts it now. Let us say it is on the pillow of his Belfast council flat just to please him; he is no longer wanting to think storm drains.

For the first few hours in the storm drain, it was horrible for him to think that he might have to put his head back into the dried mudcakes above the water line. But almost as soon as he thought how horrible it was to think that, his neck muscles had given in and now he no longer cares about what crawls in his hair. He no longer cares where his head falls back. So the old man puts his head back on the hard debris of gutter spill and closes his eyes. He remembers some things as he had always remembered them perhaps.

She comes every fortnight. I wonder what she will bring this time. I get a lot of knowledge from Channel 2. Loneliness does not exist when you have books, they are the answer to nearly everything. My worst trouble is trying to buy the books I want. I couldn't buy history of the world by H. G. Wells anywhere. This isn't a book that can be studied in a day or two. The surroundings of these council flats are kept in perfect condition. Green grass, trees, paths in immaculate condition. Now before I forget, which I have the habit of doing. I wish to mention a sister or nurse. Her name is Holland. She gave me this flat with a most beautiful smile. A smile costs nothing but what a difference it makes. Thank you, Mrs Holland. It's a glimpse of sunshine. You make it like Sun is shining.

The old man tries to shift his weight. He knows it is no good tiying to shift his weight. But it somehow makes him feel better to still try to shift his weight. A fighter? It's the everyday being laughed at, he thinks. For being small, he thinks. For being Irish. For having a head boiling with ideas. Human. Nothing, he thinks, has escaped his eyes.

If you were looking down at him from up here now, he can hardly be seen lying down there, where?

I occasionally visit the Sportsman Hotel, where in the tap room they have all the characters from Dickins hanging on the walls but one I couldn't find, Uriah Heep. I got into conversation with the habitues of this Hotel, the conversation started off with Sex which considering the age of the persons surprised me. It then led onto that god Mammon, then to houses, lawns and upkeep, buying, selling of houses. I tried to steer them onto another subject but nothing doing. Hardly intellectual would you say. I got fed up and found myself a seat and done a bit of writing like I am doing now.

One person said his wife was pregnant and couldn't get through the door. He thought this was a joke. I thought this was in damned bad taste and told him so. What respect can you have for your woman when you speak thus.

This book is about thoughts and impressions so forgive me if I shoot off to a subject that has nothing to do with the subject. Now, what subject was I thinking of?

It might have been that the old man always remembered too

much. It might have been that the old man never did remember much. It might have been that down in the storm drain he is thinking he is somewhere else. Like back in his lovely little council flat in Belfast like sitting on the lawns outside with some of his 'dear friends' like in what used to be his local pub where he would spend from ten to eleven-thirty every Saturday morning. Yes, it might have been that down in this storm drain he is now thinking he is somewhere else and is only now beginning to remember. The trains of his thinking choo-chooing on from <u>him.</u> After him? Even his eyes are finding difficulty now. He's not sure anymore what is wanted of him wherever he is now. Not even, now, from his own body and it's still warmymuddy rotting warming smells.

It's no good. The cricketers are here, (the Hotel) all dressed up in spotless white but I noticed there weren't many working class patrons. I suppose these would be out on strike or the high prices kept them away. Things must be tough for them. I got into an argument with a fellow who said that someone he knew could play any concerto, play it by ear. I said this was bloody impossible. How would he get on with the Emperor by Beethoven without the score. Treble or Bass he could play it. If I were to play anything I would need the score or would have to memorise it. I don't envy you people who can afford to attend Proms. Ive been through all that. I can listen to Beethoven, Mozart etc on cassettes but the atmosphere is missing. If I were to write a few arpeggios in front of them they'd wonder what the hell I was doing. The violin, I prefer to name by the affectionate, Fiddle, What a swine of an instrument to start on. No guide of any kind. Ah but the beauty, Later. Much later. Then the bow, Something else to learn Staccato. Watch an orchestra. All the bows go up and down together. You have to be read in Italian. Pizzicato I used to dread pizzicato. Gut strings those days, used to pull all the strings out of tune you had to allow for this. Steel strings now. No trouble.

He is retching again. The old man is retching and he also knows he is hungry. He knows his hunger goes beyond not having anything to retch up out of his stomach any more. Still the old man continues to guess which part of the sky the sun is in. If you were bothering to look down on him from up there, would you tell him? He thinks about how you didn't shine through very much for him all these months he's been back home and he begins to think about people.

Hell I wish I had some intelligent person I could converse with about books, Music. All sorts of things. People here detest good music and good literature. It doesn't matter what it is I want to know about. Is it a curse or a blessing? 1 am going to write to A.B.C. asking them to put on scientific subjects to give me something to think about. It seems to be the opinion of everyone that when one gets old they get stupid. This is not my opinion. I have plenty of room in my brain for different subjects and I want to use this room. There is a nurse down at the hospital who plays the Flugal Horn. This is the only instrument of which I have no knowledge so I will have to find out something about it. Is it treble or bass clef? It isn't played in an orchestra or I'd know about it.

Still he continues to guess the time in the back of his shrewd little eyes searching the sky, not thinking of the sky or the time. Coming on children's time. Coming on after-school time. But after the first six or seven times they had come and gone and not returned his cries for help and not returned with what they might have promised him, the old man had given up counting the time when they would come. And the days. Now only the minutes left.

25

He used to hear the sirens far-away of a large city beyond the park around the storm drain overandaround him. They were far far away when he heard them and he didn't know whether the sirens were for ambulances or fire brigades or police. But he used to prick up his little old ears when he heard the sirens far far away of a large city beyond his park.

He doesn't sit up anymore, thinking of the children. He knows those sirens are not coming for him anymore, thinking of the children. He no longer hears the sirens of a large city of people people people far far away.

My head is boiling with ideas. The Atom will allow our minds to live. I don't suppose it's much of anything much, my thinking. It's all up there. It's all up there past the stars and the hemisphere and the universes. The nebulae. But I will tell you more about that in a later book 1 have yet to write. I will write about the seven thousand star systems and the exploding Sun theory. The seven thousand are only counting the ones they can see of course. They're wonderful things, microscopes. 'Micro' meaning measuring small in Roman and 'Scope' meaning what you've got in front of you. Not many people know that. Microns, what they measure microscopes in.

I married the wrong woman I can tell you. Her illegitimate daughter bought a derelict house in Belfast outskirts going south. My God, everything was wrong with it. Drains, roofs, cement work, everything, I worked myself into bad health over it. I was nearly 65 years of age then. At last I had to pack up. My health wouldn't take any more. They threw me out then so I went into the hospital (repat). This illegitimate daughter had a write up in the paper about how he was taking care of his parents. The doctor in that repat hospital had plenty to say to this daughter, all unpleasant. This bloody old house is empty now. God help the people if anyone buys it.

The old man finishes his retching. Sour and heart-burning the initial days. Retching is only a matter of tokenism now. What do I mean by that, writing here? The old man doesn't know his veins are pulsing out large on his forehead. Purple and throbbing. The blood having risen almost to the surface. So little holding it back now. The pearl cord of his dribble pendulums from his chin. There are no mirrors left now. There is no warmth left in the world now to look by and see the pendulum cord dribbling. There are no more women to reflect him.

Strange. I get more information from women than men. I don't know why, they must think or read more. I am going to leave the subjects of Immunology, embrology, ecology and other such subjects and get on with something else. Perhaps later women. As I type this cassette is playing 'Flight of the bumble

Bee'. God knows how many times I've played this. Nimble fingers required there.

'Dear Sir,
I regret that you rejected my book. You perhaps have one person in you're employ that started off fully equipped. Without any training that could set up type and carry out different jobs connected with you're business without any training. Being a onetime instructor myself I have not had this opportunity of meeting such a person.

If you will look at the back of any book connected with subjects I have dealt with you will find that professors have had to consult other persons for particulars connected with subjects they were writing about and if at any time I have used their notes I have mentioned as they themselves have done.

Yours, etc.'

He has no more of that green stuff in his stomach to bring up. He calls it that. I write bile, or shouldn't I? Apart from the flares of his own rotting smells the old man is no longer sensible to that place. De facto. His body giving up. Only his mind swaying sensate. It licks itself with memory and with nostril Now the final stage of the physical fact begins. The coughing in the Belfast damp cellar all that long lengthy ago, for example, which he has long ago refused ever to think about again.

I thought to myself I'll go out to the Sportsman Hotel, have a couple of drinks and a talk. The talk started of with Sex. As soon as this had been talked about at great length we went onto the price of houses, the up keep etc, I said to one man why don't you bring your wife in to have a drink with you. He said, she's pregnant she'd never get through the bloody door.

I was disgusted. It shows what respect they have for their wives when they speak about them thus. This was supposed to be a joke but I couldn't see it. This book is about thoughts and impressions so please forgive me if I shoot off on a subject that has nothing to do with the subject. On the walls of the Sportsman Hotel there are paintings from Dickins. I couldn't find one. That one was Uriah Heep. That squirmy bastard.

Still, the old man coughs into himself. The body is shaking its long-friend-Parkinson's-Disease shakes. The mind is trying to free itself from the body. Above where it dips away into the opaline scum, his little old torso jerks. But not all that alarmingly. The eyes watching.

The eyes watching him from the dark further in and along the storm drain. The eyes. They are not mine. They are not yours, or are they? They are not the eyes of the old man's mind watching what is happening to him down in that storm drain, no. They are the eyes that no longer scuttle in the dark leading off from him, but hold fast watching him. What eyes?

Now let's get on to houses. Have you noticed that when Australians build a house they tie it to a stobie pole. That's an electricity pole for all my Irish and other non-Australian readers. Perhaps they are afraid it might develop wings and take off. Poles there are millions of them and the beauty of any place is spoilt by them. Along the roadside there are signs and poles everywhere. My idea of beauty isn't surfers paradise. If there happens to be a vacant place anywhere they'll stick a sign up advertising some one's pills etc.

I am now going to have a go at you young fellows. Things may not look the best at present but keep up your education. This will apply and pay in the end and take it from one who knows there is nothing easy and the one who knows gets the job.

I was sent as instructor to I got fed up with this and asked to be put on something else. They gave me about 12 men. I was then supposed to put a cable right around the 'drome. They must have picked out the laziest lot of no-hopers they could find, All they thought about was getting up to the canteen for tea. I made arrangements with officer in charge of cookhouse to supply a bucket of tea

29

every morning and afternoon. I said, right one man collect the tea, one go for cakes etc, from canteen, if there isn't more work done you're all on a bloody charge, That got them moving.

His eyes still cannot adjust to the light in the storm drain. Now he has given up trying to see. In. And down. It seems to him 'in and down' where the drain sweeps away into a sheenless black. It seemed 'in and down' for the first few days. But he hasn't had a thought like that for days now. Besides his eyes have given up trying to adjust to what is in that sheenless black in and down from him now.

The old man, too, has become accustomed to the noises. He knows the steady rhythms of the water dripping in the many resonant places somewhere around his body down in that sheenless black of his storm drain. He knows the tinny echoes from down in there. He knows the empty sounds, the hush-hush rush of the bad air.

He knows what the scratchings, the water movements, the squealings are. He used to know. Now he doesn't think about them.

He used to know what the eyes are that gleam out at him from down in there. Coming closer. From down in there. He has forgotten them, has he or hasn't he?

The greatest thing that ever happened to you was the ability to think. Hold these thoughts captive. It has taken thousands of millions of years to build a brain like yours. Use it. There isn't a damned thing that you want to know that can't be learned. You make the time and the mental partis is up to you. Just think about this. There are certain islands that have a luxuriant growth. The seeds were

30

blown by the wind or the excret of birds. The people who own these islands are making a fortune in fertilisers. The world is seething with life. Some of you will find out to your cost. You have a bath or wash. You think you are clean, When you are finished bacteria takes over again. Look at youre skin, it looks clean but put it under a high powered microscope and you will be surprised at what you see but you have one consolation bacteria live on each other so the ones that are likely to harm you serve as a meal for the others. There will have to be mutations. If these mutations are not of advantage they will be destroyed. If you want to visit other planets you will have to travel faster than light. We have had great men thinking things out, in the majority of cases they have met with nothing but abuse. I have written this in the hope that you will understand what I am trying to say.

The old man knows
the eyes were the rats' eyes.
He knows the rats are starting to edge closer. In the first days he devised way of killing them when they came close. He could improve clubs then. When the water had been higher so that it reached over his belly, they had to swim to get near him. They were easy then, the rats were. I can write this about the rats now, I think.

But now the water had receded. The rusty stain around his body where the storm drain's water had lapped for most of the first days. Now the weight on his legs was just beginning to show above the receded water line. Now the rats could approach along the drying mud sides of the walls of the drain. They knew they could jump onto the islands of debris just beginning to show out of the receding water on top of his legs. Now on dry ground the rats were something different again. It's all become something different again.

I have told you this book is about thoughts. Allow me to wander on further. Commas, full stops, I couldn't care less. Please bear with me. This is like the foetus. Starting life. Starting life all over again, The foetus (use with care). That I would say is why we have so many idiots. Care has not been used. You want filth. Come overseas with me. I'll show it to you. Rue de Ramlah, Helepolis. Skin St. Marseilles, France.

To the Creator of all things. In our ascent we have had a long climb we have gone through hell. We are in desperate need of help now, Cybemics (Freedom of choice) is of no use to us now. We need your help and PITY. When we are old and helpless take us unto Y OU without suffering. When we were young we could stand the long ascent but now I am old, I have freely confessed my sins, Now I need YOUR help. Do not need an intercipient. I speak to YOU. Not through a priest, etc. This country needs a governor general like I need pilles (haemorrhoids). Your politicians, What a shower of excreta, these people couldn't handle a chicken coop never mind a country, who put these fools in power?

In the first of these days
when the rats had to come through the storm water the old man didn't care much how much they bit or tore at his hand and arm as he held them under until they floated lifelessly away. But now his hands are swollen up. His little old hands have been swollen up for a long time now, so he doesn't feel much with them now. He thinks it is only the beginnings of Parkinson's disease, or was I just writing that? The flat the warmth the comforts, he is remembering only these now. The weight of a lifetime of people people upon him. But,

the old man has noted with his own eyes how the eyes have

come closer and hold his steadily and do not scuttle away like they used to when he coughs.

I used to speak 5 languages, Alas through not using them I have nearly lost their use. This is a pity, especially Gaulic. You will no doubt wonder why I should make a fuss about Gaulic, well I'm an Irishman. sIt's my mother tongue. I have travelled all over Ireland, Scotland, England and Wales. I can get on with anyone. I have never looked for trouble but I have never run away from it. Raison de mes etre, (there is a reason for my Existence), On my way to the dining room I passed a man lying on the ground. He had had a fit. I couldn't help him. I am not fit enough myself to help anyone. I can only sympathise.

Now I will have to leave this for a while. I must get on with the origin of life on Earth...

Often the clouds above the old man have cleared right away. This has always been at night. All the stars near and far... But mostly the days have been grey. Occasionally, I write, above him, above the old man, there are patches of blue sky and a growing brightness as though someone was taking his hands away slowly from the light. I put in a metaphor there. I have imposed a metaphor on the dying of another man. It is the height of being fatuous. Not meant. And

growing warmth, as the sun slowly comes out at the occasional time. The old man feeling the sun, the sun of his memory, the sun of Australia, the sunsong of his warm memoiy-beats, opening, tracting towards him at last, towards the opening up there above him. His sun, his sun Australia. It did not shine through to him very much in all these last months. And in all the days the old man has been down the drain the sun still does not shine directly down in on him. Never through the opening above him down in on him. The face part of his body uplifting itself in worship in automaton. The old man's face in automatic uplift for the halo shine. The sheenless dark. And now* today, the afternoon wears on the same. The old man's body cries out against the dull grey of it all. But his mind does not move. What can I write beyond what would have been observedly happening to him?

I was doodling about, a young fellow asked me if I would compose a piece of music for him. I asked him a few questions such as if he knew what piss meant, he said yes it meant plucking the strings. I started on a sonato for him. Unfortunately I left out expressions such as andante con sastenuto, largeto, largo. I had to alter the time from 3/4 to 4 in the bar. I hadn't time to finish it so what I have done is a promise of what is to come. I will compose an overture for him, can't use the typewriter for this.

Belfast, two Gods, Protestant and catholic. The people are to one or the other that they may kill or devestate much as possible. The ministers or priests contribute to this, all sense of values have gone to hell. To the detriment of poor people.

The eyes.
The eyes in the sheenless dark down in there.

The old man's little large brown eyes dart in their body for a moment. To us it looks like panic. Does the old man let the agitation in his mind lie back? He recalls at least, we say, what he is thinking.

I'll get back to myself. I hope you'll be interested. I was

bom in Belfast, what a hell of a city to be bom in. My father was a ladies and gents tailor and as I think back what a hell of a job this must have been with the clothing ladies used to wear in those days, Riding habits and so on. The gents were just as particular, the clothing had to bear the stamp of being hand made. My mother was an upholstress. We had a woman to do the cleaning etc. As soon as I was able to think my mother took me in hand, She taught me to read and write. She made arrangements with Christian Brothers to teach me. I must have been awfully young then. So off I went to Christian Brothers college all dressed up in Kniker Bocker suit. White stiff collar and college tie, My way to school was a Protestant infested area. I was easy meat for them. I was in a hell of a state when I got home. My father whom I thought didn't know I existed said, I'll see to this. He hired a retired boxer to teach me and he taught me all the dirty tricks of combat. After a fortnight of this I said I was now capable of looking after myself. When I met these louts again they must have thought they'd run into a storm. I didn't wait to be attacked then.

A shadow passes across his face. The old man opens his eyes. He does not move his head. His eyes are looking upwards.

The shadow is a bird.

The bird refuses to come into focus for his little old large brown eyes. It is a big bird and it reels in the sky above the storm drain's opening above him. He tries gently to follow it with his eyes. The great bird swoops lazily in big loops. The great bird is riding on the wind. Unfirmed and unfixed. The old man's eyes are trying to bring it in to focus. I write that for an instant the old man longs to bring it in to focus.

35

He cannot see it is only a crow. He think the bird is an eagle or an albatross. Or a great black swan on display on the wind. Now the old man is where everything is possible. All is meaning. The All is direction. He is thinking of the early dawns. The sunshine on his days in the early dawns.

We had a Bord piano at home and my mother wanted me to learn this but no, I wanted the violin. Why? I don't know. My mother bought me one of the cheapest Fiddles she could find hoping I'd get fed up with it. But, no I stuck it out and spent hours and hours of practice on this cheap instrument. In the end she relented and bought me a good one. Now I really got going, but before that my Father said can't you quieten that thing down. I went into an empty room, Put a mute on the bridge and went at it. This was now beginning to sound like a violin and not somebody trying to kill the cat. I'll come back to this later. School now. I said to the pipil seated at the small desk next to me, What is it the Brothers carry hanging from their waist. He said that is what is called a tawse and if you don't learn your lessons they use this on you. That was enough for me I got my head down and studied. I wanted no part of tawse.

This Tawse was strips of leather with a handle. It was a fearsome looking thing. A Brother I remember Brother Sweency carried on with me right through to Matric. A truly good man. A favourite saying of his was: I am teaching you a lesson but I do not want it repeated like a parrot. I want individualism. I was also going to a first class violin teacher and what he didn't know about the fiddle wasn't worth knowing, My father said to me what are you going to do now?, I said I'll have a holiday on a motorcycle. My father took me to a m/c shop and said pick out m/c you want. I picked out a Norton. I wasn't old enough to get a licence so my Father had his faked up for me.

The old man's eyes in his body continue to look up at the sky for the great bird, but the heavy black cloud has come over again.

He does not blink.

The few branches that he can see high up there kick and lurch with a sudden squall. I can write that. That the old man's ears in his body's head pick up the hiss of rain as it hits the earth around him. Don't they, doesn't he? The wind in rush-time among the leaves outside and up there. And, I can write now, that

the first drops of the last approaching storm for the old man now fall on his face.

They, the drops, start slowly. Shall I put a sense on them and say they almost seem reluctant? One by one, then, they seem to combine (what do you say?), then split up again becoming gentle and, we will write here, *reluctant* again.

The rain drops will combine and seem to harden again soon. But for now we are letting fiction lick the wounds of the old man. He is thinking. He is not there. There are no wounds there anymore, for the old man is still thinking.

I travelled all over Ireland, Scotland, Wales and England, 'Beauty', there is nothing like it in Australia. After my father said again now are you going back to school again, I said no I am going to be a plumber. To say that my parents were dumbfounded would be to put it mildly. If I thought plumbing was easy I had to start thinking again. It

37

was (a highly skilled) job. It required a lot of study but there was night school and books. If my Mother was to see me sitting still she would say aren't you reading a book, Books we had shelves of them on all sorts of subjects.

The last storm for the old man is taking its time in coming. I am giving it a personality because we have said it wants to lap at him first. The old man waits for it instinctively. He does not blink as the first drops explode softly on his face. It comforts him. The old muscles in his face relax. Cold and real and not too cold. His body thinks, come on rain. I write that his body yearns for the last rains. Let the rain come on.

The rats are coming on; let the rain come on.

Beginning of 1918 I tried to join the R.F.C. When I stated on form I was Irish and an R.C. they threw me out. This was in Liverpool. My mother had the stupid notion of going to U.S. The submarines scared her off. I started my plumbing career in Liverpool and was apprenticed to an elderly man. God he was clever. He knew everything from laying a foundation to the complete installation of a heating system. I couldn't have learnt from a better man.

And if it rains the children may not come. The children might be kept indoors and might not come on. If it rains. If it rains good, listen for the tell-tale rumble and water-rush from down in that sheenless dark down from the old man in there. If the gutters flood, if the waters come flooding on, listen for the tell-tale wave that might wash away the weight pinning the old man's legs down. That is not only my writing wish. The old man's body, I can write, is willing the final water-rush.

Let it wash down over the legs again.

Let it sweep away the rats again.

Let it cleanse the air again of fleas of mosquitoes of the mud packs where he is laying his head.

The old man's throat sings in his body, the first drops of the last storm plop-plop-plopping on his little old face. He does not know what he is singing or why, does he or doesn't he? Let me write as though he was in a stage play and we the audience and drama with internal tension is needed... so I will write here that the old man sings a song from childhood, from where else?, in a small lilting childhood's Irish way, alone and pathetic:

> There was an old man in a barge,
> Whose nose was exceedingly large,
> But in fishing at night,
> It supported a light,
> Which helped an old man in a barge.

While the old man's mind remains in his own humming.

I joined the R.N.A.S. as an Irishman I was not compelled to join anything. What made me join I don't know but they were calling out for volunteers so I thought I'll have a go. I was living in the country so do something for it. I was sent to Codfort. What a bloody awful place, This was in the middle of winter, Snow, ice, everywhere. I was given a rifle and bayonet and we had to run along and stick these bayonets in sacks of straw. I thought to myself what the hell am I doing with a rifle and a bayonet, I'm supposed to be in the Air Force. Navigation at night with the aid of a lamp, kero lamp. There is one thing running around with a rifle kept one warm but the cold in the tents was deadly. In the morning your breath would come out as steam. Cold fish for breakfast and Maconochie stew for

dinner and fish again for tea. I thought I must be mad to
volunteer for this, but worse was in store for me. After all
this I was sent up to Roehampton where I was taught
about kite balloons, How to get them up and how to get
them down. After this training I was sent to Sheemess and
was put on a cruiser HMS Mingarry, Supposed to be
looking for Subs. Never seen any. This cruiser seemed to
want to go to the bottom and stay there. Now we had to
get the balloon down, This bastard of a balloon wanted to
go every way but the right way. Of course the boat was as
usual performing up and down, But this balloon had to be
tied down, 'Done'. Another day over. Thank God I never
suffered from sea or air sickness. On the move again
shortly after that.

The rain sings into the storm drain. The rain has started falling
hard. It will soon ease for a time. But now it is falling hard,
singing into the old man's storm drain, dancing explosions on
his little old face. Flurrying the surface of the scummy water
in which the old man lies. He does not see it like that with his
face automatically turned up in ululation. Beatific? Perhaps. I
am not writing here to deny it.

His mind continues sipping.

This time Farnborough. Parachute training. Jump out and
hope the thing has been carefully packed and that it will
open. Youre either a very good liar or there is something
wrong with you.

Now that I have been trained it's France. Up goes the
balloon with camera and then all hell is let loose. The
jerries throw everything at us and the Tommies are
cursing us to hell for all the disturbance we are causing.
I'm not worried about anything but the planes which I

40

know will soon be over with their blasted incendiarys. Before we were shot down, I thought where shall I land, there is a lot of wind, when I bail out where shall I find myself. The wind is blowing away from us so I know I won't find myself in the German lines.

At last the powers that be decided we had had enough so was ordered back to base, we were stripped of tunics. All clothing was put in a steamer and we were ordered to close our eyes and dive into a creosote bath. That was to get rid of the lice. We of course had our hair cut. We were then put into a covered truck, on the sides was painted so many horses, so many men, The floor of the truck was covered with straw. We were warned. NO LIGHTS. We were carried right through Italy to a place named Taranta, We stopped at different places to use toilet and get tea and the usual maconochie stew. That man machonochie must have made a bloody fortune out of this stew.

The rain sings into the storm drain. The last rain has started to fall hard. It soon will ease for a time. But now it is falling hard, singing into the old man's storm drain, dancing explosions on the old man's face. Flurrying the surface of the filthy water in which the old man lies. The rain, this rain.

The rain, this rain disturbing the smells which he cannot smell any longer. The old man only wants to smell himself now.

The rain, this rain agitating the eyes that are watching him from down in there. I write so that you can agree with me that they are the eyes of the rats. The rats moving away to higher ground, for it is raining again. But still the old man can hear them itching. He has closed his eyes again and is smiling to himself. Nothing is how it was anymore.

We got on a boat at Taranta. It was absolutely crammed with jews. What the hell use they'd be I don't know. One jew cleaning his rifle got the bolt out and didn't know how to put it back again so I put it in for him. Didn't know where we were going. Rumours flying about all over the place. We started off I think it was going to be the middle east but I couldn't care less. The Japanese navy escort was with us all the way. As soon as I sighted de Lessops statue I knew where we were, Port Said. We were allowed ashore and there I had my first view of the Egyptians. I doubt if I ever seen, in all my life such a lot of filthy, poverty stricken wretches. They didn't seem to like us very much but they would sell to us and they struck a hard bargain, anyway all the stuff was fakes. Turn it upside down and it was marked, Made in Birmingham...

Occasionally the old man felt quite comfortable down in his storm drain. At least I can write that because I know he is thinking/writing that he is feeling comfortable wherever he is in his memory. Not here; not in Australia. No, nor now but then. Yes, sometimes he has felt quite comfortable in his storm drain because he was still alive at least. Sometimes he was thinking it could be worse: I am living, it could be worse. He doesn't think that now.

He would have to know where he was to think that now. Only, occasionally, does his body tell him where he is now. When it does, it doesn't hurt him too much now, to know that. When his body has told him about the here-and-now of the storm drain, he has felt that he has the numbness.

And at least when the numbness has been on him, he is not feeling that he is dying. And when, at times during the last few days in particular, he has thought that things could be worse

42

despite what his body has told him, he forgets how he got down the storm drain. He only remembers other ways alongthrough his life by which he could have got down the storm drain. The long road, yes or no?

I was sadly disillusioned by this time. I had had enough of wars, that blasted stew. I thought that if one has to catch a disease this is the place to get it. Flies. They must come from all over the world to get here. The natives had them clustered around the side of the mouth and each comer of the eyes...

The rain stops suddenly. It will start again soon. For the moment it has stopped suddenly. A thousand crystal taps running, tinkling, all around our old man. They are my similes. The old man is not thinking that about the rain stopping so suddenly. This is the quietus of prime movers.

The old man opens his little brown old eyes. Half of his mind listens for the tell-tale rumble and water-rush, but it knows there has not been enough rain as yet. Half of his mind tells him that. The other half of his mind tells him that farmers need more rain for their crops. Why do we have to write that?; We smile in slow amusement because we have all said it one time or another. The lapping and the lapping and

the lapping of the thickening water next to his ear, the mosquitoes shrillingly back into flight. You prickheads, he calls them and laughs. He thinks he does.

The mosquitoes are feeding off him lazily now.

Beyond where his legs stretch out, the rats' eyes return to their former vantage points. For the rain, this rain has stopped.

We were stationed for a while on the other side of the canal. This at one time was an engineering works and I suppose was for the repair of the canal or ships. Outside the engineering works was the Saina desert, Not quite sure of the spelling of this desert. All I know about it was bloody unpleasant sand that got into everything. Occasionally the bedouins used to visit us I stayed well away from the camels, the camels always seemed to be chewing something, what it was I don't know, They got nothing from us and grass certainly wouldn't grow there, What the bedouins lived on I don't know. If dirt is picturesque they were the last word, the camels loaded up with what looked to me like blankets and all sorts of things. The camels didn't seem to like things, They done plenty of grunting and they stank to high heaven.

There wasn't, not that I could see, any brothels in Port Said, but the officers must have found something. They went there every evening. The lay out was this. There was a car to take you to the jetty and then a boatman, for payment, would take you across the cannel to Port Said.. There was one cinema and a pianist who knocked hell out of the piano, nearly always out of tune...

(The old man letting his mind indulge in what he has just been dreaming about; he is lying in his dry and warm council-flat bed letting the tired visions of the night just gone dry out.)

We were there with these blasted kite balloons in the event of any Sub entering the cannel. I won't mention the name of this Capt in charge. He was more of a hindrance than a help. I had enough of balloons so I got myself transferred to Alexandra. From there to Cairo. Plenty of life in Cairo. While there they asked for an N.C.O. volunteer to escort some stuff from Alexandra to Cairo. I volunteered so back I went to Alexandra. I noted the length of the train and the fact that all the trucks were of steel without any covering' so. I thought this is going to be a damn hot ride. The goods in the train were supposed to be secret. I pointed out to the officer that one man in charge of this train couldn't look after all this length but all I got was we can't spare any more men so on I got, having had plenty of experience of Egyptian nights I took plenty of blankets with me. I had plenty of company. (Flies).

The mosquitoes are feeding off him, lazily still. I am writing that all his life has been a dream. He could never remember ever feeling set fair. There was always the side to him that wanted to sleep. Sleep. Everytime he awoke the old man didn't know at first whether he was truly awake or still dreaming.

Now, down in the storm drain, he does not care which is which.

The old man no longer thinks about how he might have come to be in the storm drain. I am writing about suicide, I think. The old man would not think of that in his warm bed and the TV and his cassette purring, all in unison, at him. With him? No. I prefer to write that the old man prefers to chuckle now. It is a chuckle that his little old body does, relaxing against his mind.

The driver of this train seemed as if he never wanted to get anywhere and at this speed it seemed as if we would never get anywhere. I am a crackshot so I let the driver have a bullet just above his head. The driver came running down to see what was the matter. I said I want this blasted train stopped every 4 hours to enable me to

45

get some tea. Told him he would get the next bullet where it hurt if he didn't stop. I would run up to the engine and fill my tin up with water from the boiler, I had tea, dry, with me, Burnt up through the day, Frozen at night. At long long last we reached Cairo. 'Phoned up sergt in charge and told him I had some goods at railway station and to send someone to take over. He said O.K. After hanging about there for about 5 hours I'd had enough so I went outside and got on the tram, The conductor came for the fare so I said Escort, he thought I said escot which means in egyptian shut up. An egyptian there who had some knowledge of english explained what it meant. I had papers and I showed them. Every thing was now all right.

For that moment then the sun comes out. The old man opens his eyes in hope. But he does not have to blink this time either, for the sun does not shine down directly into the hole of his drain. Just like it has never really shone down on him since he came back 'home', he thinks. I write here that he thinks that and, besides, the sun has now passed behind the cloud up there again.

The old man's eyes look for the big bird. They know they won't spot it anymore, but that doesn't matter. They go on searching desperately for the big bird. When

something else falls from the sky instead. The old man tries to protect his face. I can say that because his body grunts, tries to protect its face. This new thing has fallen, is thrashing on him. The old man's body gasps with revulsion. And in the meantime:

When I got to the camp the sergt said to me. Have you any money?, I said No so he took me to the pay officer who give me some money. The sergt said now that you are here why not stay a while and I did. No brothels. They had been put out of bounds by drunken soldiers who wrecked the place. The sergt said why not go to Helepolis and I did, a lovely place. A fast comfortable train, About 7 miles outside Cairo. A truly lovely place. Plenty of green stuff growing. After a week of this, Back to Cairo, I asked the sergt to 'phone up. He said Kantara. Eventually I reached Kantara, What a bloody awful place, Anything could be bought there. How could I possibly get all stuff, I went up the Nile to have a look at Ismalia. Just date trees. I went to Mesra metru. I thought the 'plane would never get off the ground, Lovely beach, Mersra Matru. On my return to Kantara c/o sent for me. I wondered what the hell have I done. I thought, 'Fanning pain into a tortured death', I waited 'til anything that had happened cooled down. It was nothing. The C/O asked me if I would accept a commission. I said no. I want to get back home.

This is the end of my exploits in world War one. Or as much as I can remember. FINALE. I will write about world War 2 later...

The old man does not write that this new thing has fallen through the hole to his storm drain. From above him. Is/was thrashing about on his face, revolted, it and it. The old man is not writing that, but he can see where it has come from and where he has come from himself and. Where this new thing and himself have both come from and he thinks.

But the tree, but the tree is itself, The Tree is itself. The tree is a Thought. Consider that. I want to talk to you all about that. The thought is a captive. Make every thought a captive. Theory of creation is Evolution. That's what it's called. I the writer have led you on to Evolution and the CREATOR of the Universe. Everything that lives comes from something else that first started hundreds of thousands millions years ago. It has been a real uphill climb with thousands not making it to what we are now. There has been no miracles. It was kill or be killed. The CREATOR meant it to be this way. To survive you had to be strong. You started of as Methane, Hydrogen, Ammonia, Water. Look at the heights you have reached since then. A fine brain. No limit to your abilities, Freedom of choice, which you have at times misused. I have given good men the power to instruct you which has also been illused. As you sew so shall you reap.

The old man now knows in himself that something alive has fallen on his face. Was it dry and hard and repulsive? Perhaps. His eyes flutter open in shock. At first he cannot know what it is. By now it has a hold on his jacket and is hauling itself out of the water. Scampering up his side. He, the old man, is still writing, he thinks (we think), in the warmth of the audience of his 'dear friends' back in Belfast. They all will read soon what he is writing for them, thinking.

Instead of abolishing a Hand Evolution demands it. You have got yourself caught up in all sorts of religion, from worshipping stones, statues and anything which an ordered mind ought to be sick about, Worship is mine and I am the only ONE who can give you absolution, If your prayers are sincere. You can pray anywhere, anytime I will listen. Look up into the sky…

The old man's little large brown eyes look up into the sky. But the big free bird is not there. But the sun is not there. His little large brown eyes fluttering up at the sky.

…you see untold numbers of suns, stars, Galaxys. All this I have made. Nothing is beyond my Power. Any suffering

48

you have now you will know peace that is beyond your imagination. This is the end of this part.

The thing that has fallen on his face now sits on the old man's chest. The old man can see its heart pounding in its chest, just under its skin, repulsively, in the eyes (I write) of the old man.

The lizard that has fallen on to the old man's chest is returning his look.

The old man and the lizard could be said to be looking at one another. Can I write that they are looking at one another with certain feelings, with certain precepts, with certain sentiments? Obviously not. But can I write that, for a fleeting moment, the old man and the lizard meet in a unity of help-me? Obviously not. But I do write that for a fleeting moment there is a stillness that is observable between them. Then the old man (I write) takes up his figurative pen for you again.

The Atom will allow us to live. Surely we will not have to start Evolution all over again. There is such a lot of learning to do and such an array of books that I am sorry I won't live long enough to learn or read enough. Here is a strange thing and yet not strange. A farmer had a piece of land, one strip of grass was always greener than any other part, he couldn't understand this. On each side of this piece of land was two poles and between these two-poles was a copper telephone wire, after a long time it dawned on him that when it rained the drips from this copper wire was the trace element of copper, In future he added this to his fertilizer. You've had thousands of years (Millions) to try this out and considering the circumstances you have done a pretty good job. There is no romance, no shooting. I was going to say no mystery but I would say the greatest mystery of all is life itself. I noted sweet smell of

Gangrene in War One. "Trench Feet". If you have any feeling of susceptibility this story will run the full gamut, Very well written.

Now the lizard has clawedscrambled off the old man's chest for the dried mud above the water line. It waits. The old man is waiting. The rain, the last rain, begins to fall again. That's good, he thinks (we think), and:

> I wish to bring to your notice several great men who were miles ahead of their time, vanLeeuwenhock, Pasteur, Darwin who were derided for their theories. They have been proved right. Computers can do all sorts of things but you cannot as yet make yourselves but Homo Sapiens can make a man or a woman each one a replica of the other but with slight differences, genes, blood etc.

With the rain starting to fall lightly on his little old face again, the old man rolls his eyes, his amused eyes, up at the lizard. He is joking, I write, with the lizard, but no words come out, I write. I am writing here that his body wants to go on. Am I writing that his body is actually starting to turn away from death now that it has this new companionship?

> Japanese; Beware these brainy, intelligent but very very cruel race of people. We have had one example in world war two, I myself haven't had any experience with these people but I have read quite a lot about them and what I have read has taught me to have qualms, in short I don't trust them. They breed and they will run out of ground to live on, They can't keep building up so what will they do, 'LOOK for room to spread'. Where? There will be no warning.

The lizard has nowhere else to go but wait by the old man's

head, in which the eyes are flirting with the lizard. The lizard, like an old man, nestles into the warm and dry and caked mud banks by the old man's head, recovering. Yes, it looks like the old man, allowing for the metaphorics of my writing.

The old man is thinking of snakes and lizards and creatures warming their cold and old veins under the hot Australian sun of his adopted country (which shows you the difference between what I would write about the old man's death and what he is thinking he himself is actually writing).

War; Syphillis; GONORRHEA: LICE. A Parade. Naked. The medical officer will inspect the parade of naked men. You are ordered to fall out, You have one of these complaints, Whose fault?, YOURS. You caught it where? The most likely place. Skin St, Marseilles, France. Anyone picking up a woman there was asking for trouble. The medical offcier lifts up your penis with a pencil, if you are of these who can't do without a woman and can pray, start praying now.

Now the lizard is trying to climb up and out of the storm drain. The old man's eyes are watching it. There is nothing there in the seeing that requires the brain's attention. The sides are too steep for this lizard, perhaps for any lizard. Each time the lizard reaches no further than the very first time it tried to scamper out of the storm drain. Now its heart pumps nervously as it gasps for breath up on the mud cakes. By the old man's eyes. (Lizard — is this Australia at last?)

I have not mentioned Crabs, their home, Hair private parts of body, Plenty in Australia, I found this out in conversation with a doctor. Common amongst the Hippie groups. There is no disgrace. Blue ointment required.

51

We are both trapped lizard and you, you look like you never gonna die, ole man.

It is still raining lightly but not enough. If it rains hard enough to wash the weight off his legs, the water-rush will drown the lizard. It doesn't matter either way, because the old man did not think that, I think. I doubt whether he would have thought that in reality. He might have had a little old pinprick of a thought about lizards — is this Australia at last?, as I have already written.

> There is no disgrace in Ascent but there is in Descent. And that is just what I'm doing, descending. This has been forced on me by circumstances and I can't do a damned thing about it, unfortunately. This urge to write these books is the last kick of a dying horse, I am looking for beauty. I haven't found it as yet in Australia. Am I in Australia at last? Perhaps I haven't looked hard enough but I think that beauty should make itself evident. I am now listening to Dance of the Hours, This is beauty, Nature had nothing to do with this except in an abstract form. Nature made the man that composed the music, Our paths are marked out for us and to say that you can by studying music become a Beethoven is just sheer stupid.

His old fingers play with the cloth that was once his coat, down where it hung in the water before the level went down a few days ago. He thinks. The old man thinks. He thinks he is writing. The cloth that was once his coat disintegrates between his old fingers. He does not think about fingering the disintegrating cloth between his fingers. If he did, we can say that he would have to think about the rottenness of the cloth that was once his trousers and the flesh of his legs underneath that. He doesn't. Does he? Can I say that where the old man's bodily functions begin and then pronoun in the same breath

52

where they might end? Or might have ended? It still has not occurred to me what tense I should be writing in when I am writing about the death of the old man down in his Sydney storm drain. Yet he still writes and thinks.

There are a good many socalled writers using words like (fuck) (shit). These to my mind should be written as intercourse, Extrecta. Perhaps this is too bloody clean for you. When I am that way inclined I will write you a filthy book, But as regards Filth I have my limits.

Now, on this time of this day, let me write the fourteenth day the old man has been down there, it begins to thunder outside the storm drain. The thunder is still a long way off. Nevertheless, one can say that outside the storm drain it starts to thunder. And now one can say that outside the storm drain the last storm for the old man is now said to be approaching.

It will not arrive for some time yet.

The old man listens to the thunder outside. He listens with one ear cocked. That half of the mind that is on the side of the ear that is cocked receives the message that there is now thunder outside. Does it, too, receive the message that the last storm for the body is approaching now? I don't think I can write that now or as yet, which?, because the old man is still thinking and writing and lounging in warmth in a place that is not down the storm drain. Yet...

yet he gets the sense of the dampness outside suddenly chilling the air inside the storm drain. His little old torso shifts as best it can, pinned down so, in automatic dislike. You (the sun) haven't shone down on him much since he's been back 'home' in Sydney, he has considered. He has never liked dampness. His little old body has squirmed so. And you never

53

did shine down in on him in all the hours and all the days and all the nights and all the thoughts and all the places where he thought he was... you never did shine down in on him, down there in the storm drain for all that time. His little old body squirming now automatically. A shudder of the life-urge.

Are the minds, morals of men to be warped, judged, by the machines or atom for the purpose of war? You ask yourselves that. It's no good me asking all these questions of you myself. Make yourselves think of such things. Deep things, You are not animals, but human beings. Think thoughts like this, Old as is the worlds vision of a cosmos and universal and had been the dreams of the unity of Nature never before has the Imagination been complete. You even rewrite that if you like. Surely you don't want me to write all your books for you.

Did mind, matter evolve out of matter, morals? Surely if. one is brave and the other fear and if Evolution means the passage of one into the other, there is no escape, therefore, from crassest materialism. If this really is the situation the lower must include the higher, and therefore Evolution is a process of climb. Fill a flowerpot with earth and plant in it a seed, at the end of four years it has become a small tree, it is four feet high; its weight ten pounds. But the earth in the pot is still there, It has not except the moiety, passed into the tree; the tree does not live on earth, nor any forces contained in the earth. It cannot have grown out of the seed, for the seed contained but a grain for every pound contained for every pound, it cannot have grown out of or from the root, because the root is still there, and at first there was nothing there but then the tree.

The thunder. Is this really the last storm for the old man? The lizard quivering with an instinct. The lizard's eyes are darting, but it has nowhere to go. Its body sways. It can feel the eyes pressing towards it from down there in the pitch darkness. It can feel the shuffles of the rats. It can sense their eyes, mean and calling. The lizard jerks, and tries to climb up the wall of the storm drain.

As I write that, you already know that it is a futile thing for the lizard to do. You know, too, then, that the lizard is a metaphor for the old man of the storm drain, even though you rejected the metaphor of the lizard and the old man.

The lizard falls down again, while the old man is thinking.

I have headed this chapter, Man, The Maker and Destroyer but you are also an intellectual, you are. With training. Trees not only do not evolve out of their own roots, but whole classes in the sea weed world have no roots at all. It is the root that evolves from the tree. Trees send down roots in the far truer sense than roots send up trees. Yet neither is the whole truth. You've got to think about what I'm trying to tell you about here. You got a brain, USE it. Everything is Nature, The World, the cosmus, and something more, Some One more. In infinite intelligence, and an Internal will. Everything that lives, lives in virtue of its correspondences with this environment. You think about that, I'm calling mothers and Fathers, Sisters and brothers too.

The lizard has fallen back down on to the old man. It turns and runs off into the down-there darkness. Where the eyes. Are. A statement stressed. The lizard flees but straight towards the rats. The old man has not seen it do this, but his little old large brown eyes watch the lizard do this. The old man hardly hears the tear-in or the squeals or the brief plunging struggle or the faint shut-off. He opens his eyes; the thunder is nearing, oh yes oh yes. But I am putting my own emotions on this just to make a better story by saying 'oh yes oh yes' — when the old man's pink ear is hearing the thunder draw nearer and his mind is *not* listening, oh no oh no. Writing the work of his workingless life still:

Evolution is not to unfold from within; It is to unfold from without. Growth is no mere extension from a root but a taking possession of, being possessed by...

Produce an organism, plant, animal, man, society which will evolve in vacue and the right is yours to say that the root lies in the root, the flower in the bud, the man in embyro, the society, organisman the family of the anthropoid ape, if an organism is to be judged in terms of immediate Environment of its roots, the tree is an earth tree but if it is to be judged by stem, leaves, fruit, it is not an earth tree. If the moral or social organism is to be judged in terms of the environment of its roots, the moral and social organism is a material organism.

Children, what children. What are you saying to me?, I hope those children do not come back. What are you saying to me?, Eh. I am writing to you, but I don't want those children to come back and taunt me. Why don't they tell their parents. They should tell their parents, When I was their age I would've told their parents about me being down here. What?! What are you trying to tell me...?

The old man realises the lizard is gone. He has just had a moment of reality about his situation down in the storm drain in Sydney where he has come back ' home' (he thought).

The moment of reality soon has past. But for a time he has remembered the children and his little old body, where it isn't pinned down by the debris in there, has squirmed. But he has now forgotten about thinking about the children. He has forgotten he has suddenly realised where he is. He has forgotten that his little old large brown eyes have been watching the lizard that has now gone. I write here that he is now trying to adjust his sight to the darkness right down there.

This trying does no good. Except that he sees the first of the rats make its approach.

The first of the rats make its approach, yes. Dramatically stated enough? Hunger its only sensation now. The old man blocking the rats' way to their normal foraging for food. Yes, this is the first of the rats moving in.

You're capacity for training is endless. Visit the library. You will see books on every subject, These were written by men, Poets, painters, mathematics, the list is endless, and the brain capacity huge. The U.S.A. have invented a bomb that will destroy life but will not injure materials, this means that all machines can be put to use immediately, this is to be preferred to the atom bomb. See how fiendish this is. I read a book a long time ago where this particular army threw some twigs into the stream, this stream flowed towards the enemy, the enemy used the water for drinking and they were drinking a drug but they didn't know this so the attackers walked in and took over a helpless army. Now, even these troops had recovered from the drug, what would happen then? Would mutation occur. Would this cause advantage or disadvantage? The affect of mutation on the genetic code could be disastrous or otherwise. This gives rise to bacterium. This could render the male sterile and the female possibly too.

Hunger wetted on the lizard and feeling its way along the scent trail towards the old man himself, the first boss rat... or should I say the boss first rat?... the first rat approaches him cautiously.

1 have in mind another man who invented another kind of bomb, this was named the bouncing bomb. On the borders of Belgium and Germany was a dam containing millions of gallons of water, the bomb burst this dam and the flood drowned thousands of innocent women and children. I blame no one. It was war in its most vicous form. At least in war when anyone strikes you, you can strike back.

I, The Destroyer, have bombed hell out of Coventry, London, Liverpool, etc. but they won't give in. I could use gas but they are prepared for this and may use it on me. I have a specialist (Van Braun) who has invented for me Buzz Bombs, V.2 Rockets. Death has sharpened the scythe and the smoke is belching out of Krupps chimneys. I have foolish men who will go into the slaughter in the name of patriotism. The Gods to whom they pray doesn't listen.

The jews: Those I don't need I will exterminate, some of the women I will use for comforts of my troops and experiments. Skins when rendered immune will be used on air force crews, Men have statues erected who ordered men into the blood bath.

The old man's eyes are watching the rat slip along the side wall and lean over the edge above his feet. The water level has fallen so that the old man's boney little feet are now out of the water. Perhaps I should have written that earlier. I have written that now. The boss first rat looking over the edge at the little old boney feet. The old man looking with his eyes into

58

those yellow and morphine and rat evil eyes and perhaps his little old mind is wondering why he no longer cares about the rats.

Then again perhaps his little old mind is not wondering why he no longer cares about the rats.

The first few times he had screamed and thrashed about with everything he had to hand. I am writing now about the very first time the old man had noticed the rats down in there. And his balls had seemed to shrink back into his belly. Can I write that?

Nevertheless, now, his little old hand goes instinctively to the place above his little old head where he has stored the pieces of wood that he has used as clubs against the rats. His mind thinking for a reality moment: was that ages ago or only my last thought?; what is this? His little old hand goes for there while his eyes look at the first rat and that first boss rat's fur and the wet slink of the first rat's fur, and his hand closes around the last of the pieces of wood that had been washed down the storm drain. His storm drain.

That had been washed down the storm drain and he had used to keep the rats at bay. But not now. The first rat, the boss rat, the after-lizard rat, the rat in front of the frozen chilling eyes of the darkness down in there, the rat of the eyes looking over the edge at his little old feet... now the first rat has come.

His hand closes around the thin end of the branch and the old man's eyes watch unseeing for the first rat to do what the other rats are watching and waiting for it to do.

Now I will come to another subject; A Primate, I had not as yet a very high degree of intelligence. I was just a rather hairy creature with no fangs or claws, A rather poor creature compared to the predators who sorounded me. I had reached the biped stage and lived on berries and small animals but could make traps to ca£ch larger animals, I was generating a small brain and enough intelligence to keep out of danger and hunt in packs.

I had by now learnt the use of fire which I got from material started by lightning, I could frighten other animals or hunt with burning limbs of trees. I had now found the way out to make myself. This I used to drive bears and other large animals out of caves, These animals being in a state of hibernation were easy to kill, With sharp pieces of stone and flint I skinned these animals and outer skins as coverings. The sinews I used for tying the skins, The caves I used for living in.

I am going to write now that the wind has changed and freshened: I hope it is right for me to write that for this one moment in the old man's time down in his storm drain. Who of us can deny that the wind freshened and changed? The rain comes harder. I wish here, too, to mix my tenses. I write a pun to you, just as the old man is writing to you, not knowing he is really down in the storm drain in Sydney, not back in his little warm and snug council flat. I write the pun: Don't get tense. Having written so much in between, that pun now falls on your deaf or death ear.

I mention this to remind you that the writing about the old man's dying can never bring home to you the horror in the old man's dying.

I mention this also to say that the rain comes and came harder, but it does not fall and did not fall to disturb the surface (skin) of the old man's face or the surface (skin) of the slicksickening sludge lapping at the old man's side.

The first rat jumps.

The first rat lands on the iron crust of weight that is pinning down the old man's little old legs down there. He swings the club. The old man swings the club. His body is still working.

But he cannot swing the club very well with his cramped- up hand and that's just his left. His right little old hand is all swollen and in fester now.

But he swings the club, but it misses the rat.

And weak. The blow is weak. The first rat turns its eyes on the little old man insolently. It turns its eyes and looks triumphantly back at the shadows, the eyes, down there in the darkness. Those other eyes. The dark bodies shifting.

The rat jumps back off him, but goes no further in retreat than the ledge from which it jumped on to him. The old man's body lies back in rest.

> Now I will come to another subject; Now that I had learnt to make fire I was able to travel about and follow animals and keep off predators. The ice age was on and animals used to travel great distances. I have only to kill to eat not destroy. By now I was learning fast, Things I learnt I passed onto my sons. The mothers taught the daughters how to scrape and make up the skins of killed animals.

The first rat looks down at the old man from its ledge. Where it has been wet... the 'it' I am writing about is its body... a line of green slime is beginning to dry. Its eyes are ohyes browner close up. The old man does not observe this, but his own eyes take in this fact.

61

But now, close up, its teeth are showing.

It moves back to the edge of the ledge above the old man's legs. Greedily.

> My sons were learning to make up flints into different shapes. On my travels with my family I meet other people like me and yet so unlike, they are not as hairy as me but seem to be very quarrelsome but they have better tools than I have. I notice their skins are sown together, not tied. Present day knowledge; This was the meeting between Neanderthal man and Cro-Magnon man and the disparense of Neanderthal man. Also the pursuit of knowledge has, it seems ceased and to find an educated man is like trying to find a snowball in hell.

> It is believed that Cro-Magnon destroyed Neanderthal species, also that Cro-Magnon were cannibals of neanderthals.

As the clouds suddenly break. As the sun suddenly comes out. But too late in the afternoon to shine down in on the old man. As the light suddenly brightens, the old man's eyes suddenly perceive. For the first time in a long time. His eyes are seeing.

Is his mind registering? Registering that You have come out to shine down, but not on him. Registering that solid rays of sunsheen spurt against the drain's wall higher up. Registering that

the first rat now comes on.

As the first rat is in the air now. Jumping for the debris pinning the old man's legs down. That slow and lazy rat arc through the air. I describe it as that thinking of my own rat experiences caught in frieze. The old man swings his gum-tree club-branch. At the rat. As the rat. It meets the rat just as it lands on the debris at his feet. The branch breaks over the rat's back. The rat rolls and tumbles into the water. It struggles there. The old man hits it with the piece of the club still in his reflexing hand.

He doesn't know whether he is hurting the rat.

The old man doesn't think of hurting the rat. I can write that for you to think that. He is doing what he is doing. And each time the water seems to soften the blow and each time the first rat seems to sink a little bit more.

Then the old man's body lies back down to rest again and the water down in there gradually washes still again where the rat once floundered. A few bubbles, that's all.

To say that when a death happens is sheer nonsense.

The CREATOR would never make all this cleverness to consign it oblivion. Don't forget you have been given cybemics, It would have been dreadfull if you had been consigned to one particular form of life. If some of you have made a mess of things this is your own fault. You have overreached yourself. For this you have only yourself to blame. You have had beauty, taste, sight, smell and the ability to cry given to you. The ability to cry I would rate number one. Relief for pent-up emotions. You are the only animal that can do that.

You have had intelligence and the qualifications to appreciate such. Instead I find you intent on destroying each other. The halt will come because you have called it. You possess all this intelligence and brains from thousands of millions of years ago you will need.

It is becoming cold outside now. The old man's little old face is blue. His heart trips at itself from a long way away. His lips are purple.

Is he suffering a mild heart attack at this juncture? No, I merely say that it is getting cold and that his lips are purple. I leave the rest up to your imagination.

The little old man's lips tingle. His hands are bitten and swollen and the colour of porphyry. I say that this is mainly from fighting the rats in the first few days. The old man is now using what is left of the club.

He is trying to lever up the debris that is loaded upon his legs there.

> The unfolding was slow but nevertheless it unfolded. What have you done with all the gifts I have given you. There is no end to your thinking. You may think yourself off the planet, Now what will I do with you? I may have given you a remission and start evolution all over again. You will be put in a corner with the cap of a dunce. This of course will come to an end but what a long end with the long intervals. Religion a dying thing.

The bit of the club left that the old man is using as a lever holds up pretty well. (Can I say that without fear of being accused of *embellishment*'!) The old man manages to wedge that remaining piece of club under one comer of the rubbish holding down his legs. He manages to push down the stick into the sludge, into the mud, the black ooze farting, down into the water until it hits the concrete bottom of the storm drain. Right down there.

Then he tries to lever the debris that is weighing down his legs. He tries to lever it loose. His mind and body are reflexing again as one again. As best they can. But can one really write that at this moment the little old man's body and mind are one...? The bottom of

the stick grates along the concrete bottom. The stick bends, but does not break. All the other so-called clubs he tried to do this with have broken. But this piece of his last club does not break. The old man's arms push on it more. He does not know he is straining to lever the debris off him with all his might, for he is writing still.

The fossils are there to prove that we came from a long distant past, this they will not acknowledge, That is why the churches are almost empty. Now they have to alliance with each other, this is a confession of weakness. This alliance will prove nothing unless they are prepared to face up to the facts. The Roman Catholic are the worst, They have statues, Burning, candles and in Port Adelaide the blessing of the water. You visit a priest, confess you're sins, You are given penance and forgiven.

This means that you can commit the same sins and you will receive absolution. I will put these prophets in front of you. Their teachings were not carried out, Mohammed, Isaiah, Jeremiah, Daneel, Hosea, Malachi, Jesus Christ, Confusius, Buddha, Gautama.

Flavus Jophus, Said in his book Antiquituity of the Jews, Jesus was a good and just man.

His little old body take a deep breath. The light spots dance before his eyes. His feelings surge back into him for an instant of giddiness and he knows that he is almost exhausted. Yet he does not seem to realize that he is straining to use as a lever the last piece of the last of the sticks he had hoarded as clubs to use against the rats.

His body gasps and the little old man pushes on the lever one last time.

The lever, the last stick. The debris pinning down his old legs lifts slightly from the vicehold of the mud. The mud farts again as the air bubbles escape. It hisses as the slime redigests the spaces. The weight has lifted one centimetre at one corner. It is just enough.

I am not being sentimental writing this. But I do insist on a little thaumatography that the debris lifted a centimetre with the last heave of the last stick. And that it was just enough.

Now the last stick breaks. The last of the weapons against the rats. But it has been enough to lift the debris enough. What rose from the opening in that split second was the stench of his own putrescence. Yes, putrescence. I write that to shock you; I do that cynically for the sake of the story about the old man, because I really know that

the old man smells and lies back. And is smiling to himself. It was sweet and his own and got him thinkingwriting-writingthinking again.

Thoughts. The heading is what everything, is what everything is about, you see something, A thought is started but you haven't the time to do anything about it now. The thought was started, Thought is the master of thinking so when you have time you will start thinking about what you have noted.

I once had this happen to me. The word Kamsa, kept coming into my mind. It had no relationship with what I was doing, I shoved it back into my brain for further processing. Several days later it came back to me that it meant 5 in Arabic, why this should come up I don't know as it had no connection with what I was doing.

The old man lying back now and his face is smiling. He is, too, smiling to himself. It's still this same afternoon. He is smiling to himself, just briefly. It is still this same afternoon and for the moment the sun has shone. It is not too late for it to shine down on him for once this very afternoon. He thinks. Smiling to his own thoughts. But slightly irritated that the sun did not seem to shine down on him very much when he came 'home', back to Sydney. Why is he thinking fantasies like that (about leaving his comfortable little council flat and returning to Sydney
where the sun hardly shone through
where his sister wouldn't want him
where his brother had disappeared
where the grass and trees were browner, duller
where his childhood was not lodged anymore)
at a writing time like this?

He is getting a bit cross at me. Our writing threads are getting a bit tangled. We have to affirm what we are doing.

One.
I am writing about the old man trapped in a Sydney storm drain.

Two.
He is writing about being back in his lovely little council flat in Belfast *where he might be,* not where I am trying to put him with my writing.

Three.
We are both writing about the little old man caught in a Sydney storm drain.

He has forgotten about me now. He goeswrites on.

> Now I will come to that parasite of the human brain, (however beautiful it is) THE BODY. Clothes to keep it warm, take the clothes off to keep it cool, if you don't excrete, Laxitives required here if not normal, urinate, in fact it seems endless the things this body wants and needs. All this is so the brain will have a good supply of blood. Without a very active brain, life would seem like hell to me if such a place as hell exists. I'm wandering away from the subject. I appreciate flowers, the perfume, beauty and beautiful music. Eugenics...

I will write that I have an eye-witness report to say

that the junk that was on the old man's legs wasn't all that heavy. Really or really?, which? A few sheets of corrugated iron sheeting, a binding of wood and bark, a mortar of pulped paper and cardboard, a sheet of asbestos probably from some old derelict building. But all caught and bound by fencing wire, and silted over, so that in actual fact the whole lies under a heavy thickness of mud. The mud had no chance of drying to dust all that time. Only

the last rain and the last water-rush would free his legs.

And the last storm for the old man was approaching. The clouds thicken again. The sun peters. His little old large brown eyes scan the sky for the great bird and its circles. But there is no bird. His eyes cannot spot the great bird. The last storm approaching.

... Eugenics. This is not a very nice subject to think about and may seem heartless but in my own case this is what I would wish to happen to me.

We have people whose brains have completely gone and for whom there is no chance of recovery and I think this would be merciful to carry under a panel of doctors. The future dares forget the past, Heredity is the guiding star, human beings the product of two factors. Eugenics is a factor that cannot be ignored. Heredity is something that comes to you from a long way back, in fact you'd need a book on evolution to get at the full facts. You are bom with a genic code and this is YOU with all you're faults and goodness. (Buddha, think evil, You are evil. Think good and you are good)

I was saying that the junkdebris on the old man's legs was not heavy. That is as ridiculous to say as it would have been to say the junkdebris was heavy. It held the old man down by half of his old body for a long enough time for the last storm to reach him. It held the old man's body down for long enough for

the children, and don't forget the children (the children who fed him a biscuit a day and a drink a day and did not tell anyone because he was their own little living doll out of TVland), to taunt'n'taint him all those days.

So the debris was heavy enough. It broke the last piece of the last club the old man had used to ward off the rats.

It was heavy enough.

In the natural course of events, nature would step in. Nature is kind. Also very cruel and you commit a grave mistake by trying to play God. There is…

Back in Belfast
he had worked on and off on the same out-of-Belfast farm for old man Moyle for thirty years, give or take. He had laboured and done the district's plumbing and laboured and slept above the stables in a room that old man Moyle had made up dry for him. For thirty years. Off and on. Then one day (as I have to write however common it is to write it), old Moyle's eldest son came up to give him one week's notice to quit the place because everybody knew that his little old fingers could not monkey wrench with the cold anymore and furthermore — the Moyle son had seen it with his own eyes —

the old man had been seen tottering with a shovel full of pig's shit. I am being perfectly blunt in the use of my language, hoping to shock you all about how circumspect I have been with my language about the little old man so far. And still the old man is writing to you as he cries his heart out to you from you-know-where.

> ... no such thing as death and this so called death is not the finale to the human beings. It was not meant to be such and the CREATOR would not have it so. The Creator being the Creator of innumerable suns, planets, oceans. It has been a long climb for the human race but hasn't been worth it, the human race has done some wonderous things and I dont think the CREATOR would wish to destroy this intelligence. The human being has beauty all over the world, PAINTING, Music. Sculpture, in fact everything that is beautiful.

The old man would like to feel his face. I take it that you recognise that this is a thought. He is thinking of the here-and-now, because he would like to feel his face. But he cannot feel his own face. He cannot seem to move his little old sinewed arm and he doesn't seem to want to try and move his little sinewy old arm, even though it would be nice to be able to feel his own face. We do not know why he would like to feel his own face. Suffice it to say that he does.

His eyes seeming so heavy and his mouth so swollen. His body's sensation crabbing around in themselves just at this moment of time. Let us call this just part of the ole routine, the old little old-man soft-shoe shuffle around his Belfast domain. Ah yes, the fruit stall first. I shall try to write immediately what the old man would be thinking right now if he had thought by himself about his Belfast routine. Two reasons why this can only remain a piece of my writing and not the realities of the old man's life... One, he is physically in deep distress right now and, two, he would be shocked were I to suggest to his face that he ever had such a let-me-live, sweetly-sick routine. However,

his daily routine in Belfast. I am writing that this is what the old man would have thoughtwritten about that:

'Out by nine, under the railway arches at ten past the half hour, fresh air and pigeons, Mrs Maunder gave me fruit if I kept the birds off her fruit stall while she went around the comer to do her morning thing, you know what I mean haha, We all have to do that and don't you forget it, I used to keep the old eye out, if anyone came I used to say Mrs Maunder is around the comer doing her morning thing, some of them used to laugh when I told them that, I don't see what's funny about that, I don't see what that's got to be laughed about over. We all have to do our morning thing and don't you forget it, I used to like her apples, your Sunshine apples she used to say to me, they've come all the way from Australia can you believe that?'

You see how artificial my trying to write about the old man on

71

my own is? I thank Edward Nugent for his insights, while the old man in our own storm drain dies that much little more, still writing to you an emission from a comfy Belfast council flat, like not half.

> You carry mound with you, Heredity. Environment. These two could be a blessing or a curse. The way people marry and have children is an insult to heredity. This is complete indifference. With the sophisticated methods they have now pain does not exist. You are helping a lame dog over the style, if you are not enthusiastic about this that is understandable but consider the circumstances. You have here a person who is just a living vegetable and using a bed that other people may desperately need. This matter requires graves consideration and in spite of you're pity deserves common sense, So strongly do I feel about this That I have donated my body to R.A. Hospital.

In Belfast
(I am still writing as I feel the old man would think about his daily routine in Belfast; you can judge for yourself how far off target either my ability to write is or fiction is when fronted with reality — we are, at least, trying to nudge the two, fiction and reality)
the old man, after Mrs Maunder's fruit stall, is in dwarfish lurk around the back of the Great Wall of China Restaurant. This is what he is thinking about that:

'Through the shopping centre, past the Oasis cafe to see if they wanted any help with the dustbins. Mind you, I never loitered. Five to nine, exactly. Five to nine, right on the dot, guaranteed. Sometimes they kept me waiting for a bit of the old breakfast and I had to bolt it down in a hurry to get on my way. Now I don't think that was considerate. I was due down the newspaper office at ten past nine, but they still kept me waiting out the back of that Great Wall place so I had to bolt down what they gave me for breakfast. Nice and rude, you know. If they treated me as though I was one of those cats hanging around those dustbins, well the next day I didn't turn up at all. Serves them right if they felt sorry for it afterwards. Two can play that game. The first day back, I'd only touch half of my breakfast. That got at them. I bet they didn't feel like keeping me waiting the next time.'

And I am writing that back in Belfast our little old man loved to read books. He used to bore his 'friends' for hours talking about the books he read in the library next to the far heater in winter where a She had a seat always reserved for him in winter or near the window in summer where the same She kept a chair reserved for him in summer, and this is how I envisage him talking about it:

'That kind lady at the library, always a kind word. Very important that and you shouldn't forget it. She knew I wasn't in there for the warmth like some of the Elderly there. She was nice and kind, She knew what I get like when there's books about, Always like that ever since I can remember. My Mother used to say, What are you sitting around for, Go and read a book or something there's plenty of books around for you to pass the time. Now, that woman in the library was nice and kind but she had a big crooked nose just like a parrot. I didn't mind that but I couldn't look at her straight, You can't help thinking that a nose like that couldn't be very hygienic you know, Especially since she had such short stubby fingers. She wouldn't even be able to reach places where some things would get caught up in that nose. Still she gave me books and a cup of tea if I got there early. I couldn't come at that nose. I never did like her tea, but you can't complain to good friends. Just grin and bear it, always been my motto. Kindness is what makes the world go around, don't you forget it. Sometimes she'd give me a biscuit with it. Other than that, she didn't give me much, so I didn't feel too worried about saying goodbye to her to come back home at last. I used to take her a pear now and again, Always pay your debts, too...'

I have paused and I am now writing about the old man's next stop on his daily round — the newspaper office:

'In the newspaper office at nine thirty sharp. I didn't like to be late. If I was late, sure enough the tea they gave me used to be cold. Beside I didn't like to hurry on top of that tea and biscuit from the library and the fruit Mrs Maunder gave me to watch the stall while she went to do her morning thing. You should never bolt your food. So if they made the tea early at the newspaper office it used to throw me right off. And they were kind to me there, especially Mrs Hamilton. Letting me read the morning edition hot off the press. Funny she dressed like a man, I always meant to question her about why she didn't like men. To me that's definitely unhealthy in a good-looking woman.

The trouble was she had a few crooked teeth in the middle of her mouth. I couldn't look at her straight either. How can you read your newspaper properly with those crooked teeth smiling at you. Perhaps I should have told her to do something about those teeth, I don't know. Still, what can you say. They weren't my crooked teeth, I couldn't say very much about them...'

I am building up here the element that the old man became a marvellous survivor. He developed long ago the way of never showing his revulsion, but only smile and listen and wait. There is always the eternal maternity in women; he just had to hold on and wait. I write this in order to lead in to what I think the old man down in the storm drain would have said about his

74

little council flat in Belfast and the woman Miss Glamorgan who lived in a little council flat below him:

'Miss Glamorgan. Oh, *that* Miss Glamorgan. I used to read parts of good books I came across to Miss Glamorgan. She never understood a thing. They should have put her down and that really is my opinion, But she used to say you come down and watch television and she'd always have a cup of tea ready when I got down there. And a biscuit. Always one of those biscuits I didn't like but I didn't like to say I didn't like them and I didn't like to tell her that I didn't like milk and sugar in my tea...'

I am filling in here with images of the old man's past life in Belfast. If you will remember the old man in the storm drain has stopped writing as though he was really back in his little council flat back in Belfast. He lay back after levering up the debris off his feet a little way and smelt his own putrescence, and his eyes and mind are exhaustedly scanning the small patch of sky he can see for the great bird whirling in circles above him. It isn't. And while he is and while it isn't I have him thinking what I know he would be thinking about Miss Glamorgan who lived in the council flat below his. But I change the rhythm to boost the story along by writing now in the third person, removed unmoved:

In Belfast,
back in Belfast,
when the little old man started to become a character around that area, the people who he waylaid on his routine started to joke about <u>him</u> in a loving way to their dinnerparty friends. They joked about the confused snippets of information he picked up in all those books he read down at the library. But they joked far more about his one big romance.

His one big romance.

His affair of the heart with the little Welsh lady who lived in the council flat below his. Miss Glamorgan. She alone had taken a shine to the little old man who was Irish but said he was Australian and had to come 'home' back to Australia to have You (the sun) shine through down to his cold old little shivery bones again or he would surely die. If he didn't get back 'home'.

But You never did shine on him very much, did you, when he finally got back 'home'.

Miss Glamorgan. The two of them walking across the garden together. Our old man and that Miss Glamorgan. Neither of them too much in the prime of marriageable life, but who knows? And who can care.

But the old man would have to admit now to not liking Miss Glamorgan's smell really. Oh, he wouldn't tell her he didn't like her smell. He didn't tell her he didn't like her biscuits. He didn't tell her he didn't go much on having milk and sugar in his tea. But most of all he would never tell her that he didn't like how her legs were hairy and bandy.

What I must write here to tell you about Miss Glamorgan and the little old man is that she kept all his savings in a tin under bed. She knew how badly he wanted to come back 'home'. So she made him save a few shillings (then) a week and kept his savings in that tin under her bed.

No, he never did like bandy-legged women. And Miss Glamorgan had cowboy legs. He never told her he didn't like walking down the road with her or strolling across the gardens with her because he thought people they passed would be looking back at Miss Glamorgan's bandy legs and thinking, 'Look what that little old fellah has been landed with!' And he would never think of telling her he really didn't go on women who were going bald. Especially when it came to drinking that tea you didn't particularly like with its milk and sugar and finding a hair off her head floating around in it. What with those hairs floating around and her hairy bandy legs, it was all a bit much. But she did keep his shillings saving in that tin under her bed.

When Miss Glamorgan was discovered to be dead on that seat in the gardens, it was said that the old man knew that she was but just couldn't move away from her. It is not me who is postulating a real romance between them, after all. It was, after all, what had happened. She had died on that seat there and it is down on record that he sat there and wouldn't move away from her. Just looked down on her.

On account of this I am going to try to write what I think the old man was thinking when he was sitting on that garden seat looking down at the dead Miss Glamorgan next to him. And I am also going to confuse it by having him confused about where he is — on the garden seat with Miss Glamorgan back in Belfast or having a moment of clarity down in his storm drain. I write him as thinking:

'Even if she did smell a bit and even if she did make me go a bit queasy with all that hair floating around in my tea. You forget about things like that. She looked like a little doll there and I knew she was dead and the pain you can get when all you can hope for is that she went out with a whimper I didn't hear and it didn't hurt too much and how rotten it would be if she knew how I didn't like her smell and her being all that bald and her hairy bandy legs. They still look bandy. Death doesn't make you look any the less bandy. I wonder whether you stay bandy when you go to the other world after you're died, whatever that other world is and I don't want to die here either. I don't want to die. There's no reason why I should die here. I ought to be able to walk out of here without dying. I don't want to be carried out of a storm drain dead. I don't want them to have to come down here and fish me out like this. I'm home. I've come home. It's me. Don't you recognise me. This is my face. Don't I shine through it anymore? I'm home. They shouldn't have done this to me. I didn't come home to die…'

These that I write now are verifiable facts about the 'post-Miss-Glamorgan' Belfast period of his life:

The old man used to sigh heavily and bow his head when he suspected that his Belfast friends along the route of his daily round were telling the story about him staying on the garden seat with the dead Miss Glamorgan, and their great romance. He never spoke about it himself, only bowed his head humbly and flicked his eyeballs to the corners of his eyes just to sneak a peep to see if the story had some 'aw, shame' effect.

Another fact was that for two days he had forgotten that Miss Glamorgan had kept his savings in that tin under her bed for him... the saving with which he was going to return home' to Australia with. (Can we not presume from this that they actually did love each other?) When he finally did remember the savings in the tin he hurried downstairs to her room, but the tin had gone by now and the room had all been cleared out and nobody had ever, or would ever, mention anything about funny old Miss Glamorgan having savings in a tin under her bed. His saving to come back 'home'. There was only the Australian Migration Office left now, but there were regulations about the age of assisted migrants and so on and so on.

And when I bring all this up to the surface again, his mind floats neither here nor there, but *on,* like one of Miss Glamorgan's hair in his tea; the old man thinking:

'One thing I never showed Miss Glamorgan was my legs. Mine are not bandy, but I never showed her my legs. Not like hers, bandy and all those varicose veins that nearly used to make me choke on my tea in front of the television set, too. Legs like piano legs, Two fiddles etcetera and her smell and her hairs dropping somewhere you had to put your mouth. And being so upset when I saw her lying there on that garden seat and forgetting my saving under her bed. I don't want those children. I don't want those children to come back and taunt me. I don't know why they don't tell somebody I'm trapped down here. *Where?...*'

So in Belfast
he lay outside the Australian Migration Office with his little large brown waiting spaniel eyes in silent plea until someone with the authority gave in and said yes to him.

His past has now turned the full circle of my prose. I started this story of the old man's entrapment in a Sydney storm drain with him getting on the plane to come back 'home', wearing the same silk shirt that he had bought in Australia forty-five years ago. You may remember, for I am now returning to the old man lying back in the storm drain searching the patch of sky above him for a great bird that might be circling above him. Is there a great bird? I opt to write that there isn't, or, if there is, he does not see it. For his mind has left his eyes now. His eyes are watching for the great bird but his mind no longer is. Instead he is writing for you.

He is writing for you from the comfort, from the warmth, of his own snug, wall-papered and carpeted little council flat in the living heart of beating Belfast again and he thinks.

Thoughts that don't bear thinking about. My name is
Sean, John, Sharpe. This name will mean nothing to you.
I am not going to write a war book, Theres enough of
these to start another war. I have already written about the
futulites of war, I have seen beauty but I have seen a hell
of a lot of misery. More misery than beauty caused by
wars. People seem to be at their worst in wars. The
'victors' leave the vanquished with such a load of misery
and debt. This is the embro of another war and so it goes
on. When the hell are you going to learn. Hatred breeds
hatred. This is the start of another war. Humiliate him,
thats all it takes. All men will suffer only so much
indignity. He'll breed thoughts. Dangerous thoughts. Evil
begets evil. Every country is to blame. Every country is in
desperate need of Thinking men.

Back in Belfast
in Belfast in Belfast trying to get back 'home' to You (the
sun) by stealth by insinuating himself by lying outside offices
with his old brown eyes spanieling by craftiness by silent
pleading by giggling with by the giggling because of his little
living doll-ness by finger-crossing by wishing by being
pathetic by the little whinings by the little large sighs of
homesickness by cajoling by edging up towards by throwing
himself on the mercy of by sheer bathos whipped up by
making himself into an all-women's cluck-cluck

by the sheer drive of an old man's dying self now • '

but there was no one to meet him and no one to want him back
here at 'home' and You didn't shine down on him very much
at all.

Is he thinking that while writing this?

You women want to be equal of men, Are you sure you are not in evil his superior. Don't try to be like men. There is enough bloody trouble. The trouble may not show but it is fermenting. 6 lbs of stuff called I believe nervon is enough to kill as many people as would cover 2 football fields without damaging buildings. It is not affected by any kind of weather but it kills people stone dead. You have no means of knowing it's there. You have no means of knowing it's there. It can be put anywhere as a simple parcel. If you picked it up you'd probably throw it away or perhaps take it home but what ever you do it will reach the culmaniting point. Who the hell would suspect these innocent looking parcels to contain anything deadly. This is what man has thought up and you women want to be equals. Try and be Superior. I don't know whether Mona Lisa wore a smile or a sneer.

Now the second rat comes on.

It sits on the ledge above the old man's legs where the first rat had sat. The old man's body tries to shift itself automatically. It is starting to get cold now. (That double meaning of the idiomatic pronoun is deliberate.) The second rat leaps down from the ledge onto the debris that is still weighing down the old man's legs and sits there. Waiting. It is looking at him and waiting.

The old man knows what it is waiting for.

He knows that instinctively, without having to recognise the reality of this storm drain and the reality of dying in this storm drain. He lets it wait. He knows instinctively, too, that the other rats down in that pitched darkness down there are watching the second rat. He lets them wait too. It is getting too cold. The wind is tossing the branches of the English beech tree that he can see through the opening above him. It is not even a gum tree. It could have been a gum tree. I can write that because I have been to the spot where the storm drain is and have seen that it is an English beech. Not even for the sake of the story is it a gum tree. Or am I deliberately using the fact that it is an English beech tree as against a gum tree as a deliberate irony for his 'homecoming'? I don't know. All I know is that it should have been a gum tree at the very least and that now the wind is getting up and tossing its branches.

The clouds still swirling. The last storm is settling on Sydney uncomfortably.

Now the second rat moves towards the old man's feet. The old man no longer tries to move his legs. Not even his body tries to tell him to do so now. He is stretching and yawning in his mind.

> Channel 2. Young lady age about 15 playing violin, Embryo virtuoso. Education common sense desperately needed. Fellow seated next to me can't read or write. Can't tell the time on the clock. In my opinion not worth the food he is eating. Lots to say. Mostly nonsense. He's satisfied 'with himself'. Look this is the way I look at it; I don't give a damn, Man or women. If you know more than I do I'll take instructions from you i.e. if I thought you did. Thought is the master of thinking. Make thought a captive. Surely thought imprisoned in your brain will come up with something that satisfys or repels...

I write a little bit more about what it was like for him before he got adjusted to being down there.

During the first few days and nights he could move his little legs. Even when he couldn't feel his legs anymore he could see that he could still move his legs because he could see the toes of his shoes moving. After a time, the toecaps of his shoes did not move all that much no matter how hard he tried. Still the pain had passed quite quickly once the numbness had ceased being a feeling and there was nothing.

He wasn't too unhappy when that happened. He didn't want to remember how torturous the nerves in his legs and back had been before the numbness set in.

And anyway he couldn't see the toecaps of his shoes move anymore much. Besides there were the children to taunt him; they had just started coming around by then.

> The past dares the future; Look around you. You must have some thoughts. Something, anything. You smell a perfume. Now where did I smell that. You are thinking. You hear a note or turn on the radio or T.V. Thought. I will see if I can get that tune when I get home, You're thinking. I have a compouter but I cannot breed from a compouter. They can do anything. But they can't make their own kind, but you can, with a very slight difference. FINALE. I am writing this in the hope that students may learn something from it and constructed as we are they have one hell of a job.

I am writing again of the old man down there in the present. When his little large old brown eyes look up again, the second rat has stopped by his feet. When his hand raises itself, the second rat doesn't even bother to move. When his old eyes looked he found to their surprise he had not raised his hand. He only thought he had, if he was thinking about it at all.

The old man is now looking at the hand he thought he had raised. He has turned his dimming conscious light on the fact that he is down the storm drain in Sydney and that the hand he thought he raised has not moved. He raises his hand again. It doesn't move. His hand does not move.

His hand feels like it is raised above his head, but the second rat has not moved and suddenly, again, he does not care anyway for he is now no longer, again, down in the storm drain there.

'The future dares forget the Past'. Heredity is the guiding star, human beings the product of two factors. Eugenics is a factor that cannot be ignored. Heredity is something that comes to you from a long way away way back, in fact you'd need a book on evolution to get at the full facts. You are bom with a genic code and this is you with all your faults and goodness. (Buddha; Think Evil, You are evil. To think good, You are good.) The future dares the past. Nature would step in here...

When he looked up, the second rat has stopped by his feet. When he raised his hand at it, his hand hadn't moved. When he looked his hand hadn't moved. The old man's eyes are now looking at the dead hand that he thought he had raised to scare off the rat sitting on his feet. His body wants to raise that hand. The nervous system spurts and the old man's metabolism drives into counter alarm, but still the old hand does not move.

The second rat is becoming agitated. Behind it the other rats begin lining the mud paths on either side of the water channel down in the storm drain. The eyes have come and are looking at him. The eyes are watching the second rat, too. The old man's metabolism ceases its panic. It sees the rats are not bad looking. It sees that perhaps they have come to caress him at last. Perhaps, his body tells the old man, they have come wanted at last. Soothing now.

Nature is kind. Also cruel and you commit a grave mistake by playing God. There is no such thing as death and this so-called death is not the finale to the human beings it was not meant to be such and the CREATOR would not have it so.

I am repeating all this so that You may listen, and learn something, You've got to use your godgiven brains or you are NOTHING.

The CREATOR being the CREATOR of inurable suns, Earth, Planets, Comets, Oceans. It has been a long climb for the human race but they have done some wonderous things and I don't think the CREATOR would destroy this intelligence HE has made, You're works are exhibited all over the world in the form of Painting, Sculpture and Music. In fact everything that is beautiful. You carry around with you, Heredity and Environment, These two could be a blessing or a curse. The way people have Intimacy they certainly don't care about heredity or there would be such a lot of fools around. This is the curse of indifferent people. If they are such that they carry this heritage around with them someone will have to take over.

The old man raises his head. (I say that because the effect, whether the old man is willing his head to move or it is only neuro-motoring, is the same from our vantage points of observation.) But when he looks up his little old eyes are still looking up at the sky through the opening above him.

His head is not raised to look at all the rats lined up along the dried mud ledges above his legs. No. Instead they squint.

As they, all eyes, look down on his legs and the second rat moving in now not so cautiously. He is looking up at the unforgiving sky up there. It is starting to rain heavier now. It must have been raining for some time now for a gully of water is starting to cascade down into the storm drain from up there.

It falls on his upturned face. He does not move.

> With the sophisticated methods they have now Pain does not exist. You are helping a lame dog over a stile. If you are not enthusiastic about this that is understandable but consider the circumstances. But you have here a person that is just a living vegetable and using a bed that other people may desperately need. This matter requires grave consideration and in spite of your pity deserves common sense.

> So strongly do I feel this that I have donated ray body when I am dead to anatomy section of the Hospital to do as they like with it and in the hope that students will learn something from it and constructed as we are they have a hell of a job learning. Consider the brain...

This passage is his thoughts/writings over, while his old eyes shift to see the rats lined up there. His thin peeping consciousness on reality tries to remember raising his head so that he could watch them better. But his veiny head has not raised itself. His hand is still floating swollen and mush-damped on the top of that gluey water there. He tries to raise it. It floats still. The old man is still looking upwards at the unforgiving sky. He does not know he is any more.

> ... brain. Look what it has done and what it can do,

86

Beauty, devastation, Warmth, Cold, Tenderness, Brutality. Man 3 lbs of it, Female slightly less but not much less but I would point out Multa sed Multium (Quality not Quantity). I think the greatest mistake Nature ever made was making up bipeds instead of quadrupeds. The heart has to pump the blood all the way down to you're feet and to make sure that the blood does not return it has non return valves in your veins.

Somehow the old man has managed to lift his right hand. It wavers in the air in front of his face. He has a side thought that it may never come down. (I offer that as a fictional possibility.) The right hand is not floating any more. He is lifting it. It is huge on the end of his thin little blue nobuled wrist.

The rats shift and watch. This prose comes in waves.

His right hand is being watched by his own eyes and his own thin bubble of consciousness of being down there in the storm drain and by the rats.

The gully of rain water now pouring into the opening above him and waterfalling onto his fun-making little old face. His hair in gloss as the water begins to wash some of the mud from it.

With a shock we perceive that it is bringing out a recognisable human being from him to us. But we are sentimental because we are fellow human beings. The rats are different; they are not sentimental. The old man is thinking of surging beauty that could be for all.

I am now going to try to teach you how to make Music. This is one of Man's greatest achievements. It can bring beauty, tenderness, companionship, gaiety, Its beauty is endless. I suggest you buy a fiddle, (fiddle is an affectionate name for) Violin. It is not an easy instrument to master but the rewards are great. Buy a cheap one to start with. There are 5 lines and 4 spaces. The strings are named G, D, A, E. The notes in the spaces F.A.C.E. The notes ON the lines are G.B.D.D.F. Get a sheet of music from somewhere and you'll know what I'm talking about. On the fiddle is a black piece of wood (ebony). There is no marks, The following notes are open, No fingers needed G, the next one D. The next one A. The next one E. The first finger on G string is A, the next one with second finger is B, the next one C, you're fourth finger is D. The next string is D and the first finger is E. The next finger is F. The next finger is G. The next finger is G, the next finger is A. Now the second is A, The first finger is B, The next finger is C. The next F...

The old man lets his swollen right hand fall back into the water. The swollen right hand of the old man suddenly falls back in to the water as though giving way to gravity finally. I leave either option open for you.

The right hand, as an extemally-observable happening, falls back into the water and slaps it with a sharp crack. The rats around the sides of the drain retreat, ghosted.

The second rat that was near the old man's shoes retreats.

But even the other rats have not retreated very much. They have realised that this was not a club but merely the old man's hand. (I will leave in this kind of anthropomorphising the concepts of the rats.) The wind is in the rising outside. The branches he can see, if he was seeing, now in the movement of arcs. The old man's face automatically moves itself so that the gully of rainwater does not cascade down on him. Now it splashes on the rock at the side of his head by his ear. He would be able to hear it secretively disintegrating drop by drop if he was listening.

He is not. He is more comfortable now than for a long time.

He thinks he can hear sparrows outside. And the chorusing of sundrenched magpies. Let us affirm that to give him a more knowable, human, *real* quality for us. So, the old man listens carefully to the sparrows outside and the chorusing of the magpies. And all that all that all that music in the air.

I have now rewritten my book about teaching you Music. Here it is coming up: I am now going to teach you Music. Since Man became man he has been tinkering around with all sorts of instruments. If you can't learn after following my instructions, you must be awfully stupid or deaf. If you are in any trouble I will help you. *FREE* 6, Booth Ave, Linden Park. The violin. Buy a cheap one to start with. All the Beauty, Tenderness. The rewards are great. It is an instrument with a soul. I am now going to draw out 4 spaces. That will mean 5 lines. You must remember these.

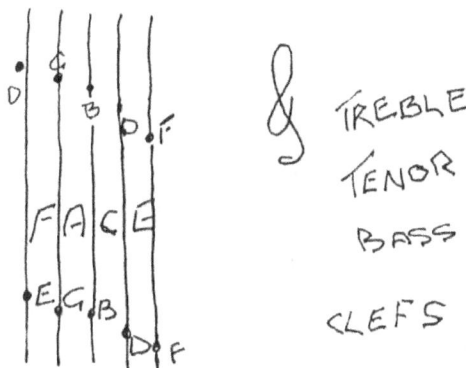

Now hold fiddle up in front of you, Small piece of wood at bottom is tail piece. This tail piece should have small screw for fine tuning. You need this and if one is not fitted get one fitted. If any trouble get shopkeeper to phone me, Belfast Flats, 6 Boothe ave linden park. Names of strings are AE, right side, G.D. left side. Notes. Spaces. FACE. Lines, EGBDF. Don't forget, any trouble, come and see me or 'phone I have never had a pupil yet that failed.

I will help you at first FREE, afterwards when you become a little proficient will charge you one pound per Hour...

I will continue to write that the old man is listening and is hearing meaningful things, even to him.

The old man listens and hears the chorusing of the magpies. He is listening carefully and hears the seagulls not too far away. He hears the seagulls and knows that they must have come into land. That there must be strong weather out at sea. The storm.

The last storm.

The old man hears the hush-hush of the old gums in song. He listens carefully and hears the rumble of distant thunder. He hears and listens carefully to the siren of a distant ambulance. What does this mean? Rescue or symbolic? It does not matter which; the old man has given up any hopeful thoughts because his mind is no longer down in the storm drain really. Even so, I am saying he listens to the ambulance siren fading away. He is listening carefully without moving his head any more.

He does not know just yet that the rain will soon abate yet

again for a while. For, while they lurk back to the shadows,

the children are to come.

> Thoughts on the Futility of war. Helopolis, Egypt. Started
> off with brand new Wellington. After test was declared
> O.K. Loaded with fuel, Ammo for Malta. Lovely
> morning. Give pilot course. Got to Malta. They had to
> shove some Spits out of the way so we could land. Malta
> was in a hell of a state. Got the stuff off and started for
> England. Half way, got a radio message from England.
> Germans playing hell over Channel and south of England.
> Plotted new course over Holland,' gave it to pilot. Lots of
> flack over Holland but couldn't reach us. When we got
> over Dover all hell let loose. Another radio message
> Gatwick fogged up. I asked how about Biggen hill. No
> good, Fogged up. I asked the pilot if he had enough fuel.
> Not a chance. Well theres only one thing. Hendon.

The gully of rain water slackens off its spill against the head
of the old man. The vaporous layer outside above the opening
deepens to oppressing. The old man's body tries to hold its
breath. We don't know why it tries to do that. What we do
know is what it is not —namely nervous expectation. If you
like, dread. It isn't that. I think I can write that it is a holding
of the breath by way of asking the rhetorical question: 'Is this
it then?'

Outside, everything seems to be holding its breath, too.

This is the last pause now.

The old man does not know or care that this is the last pause
or that it will not last long. He thinks instinctively that the
water-rush is not too far off now. It will come quickly when

the last storm really bursts. Soon everything called All This will come to an end for him. His little old large brown peepers look up towards the opening above him. No, he is not looking at the sky to see if You will shine through today. He is not looking up at the sky to see if the great bird is circling there now. He is looking up at the flicks of grass glistening with rain drops, heavy with rain dew, bending their weighted heads into the opening to the storm drain above him.

Stillness.

The rush has paused for a while. For the children to come.

> We got to Hendon and there were planes all over the place. I said to pilot get higher. No reply so I went to see what was the matter. One pilot had incendiary bullet through both legs. There was a hole beside other pilot. It looked as if a cannon shell had knocked him out so I couldn't for him. I set 'plane on auto-pilot and had a look at second pilot. He was groaning a lot so I went to first aid box and got a needle and filled him with morphine through the thigh. That quieted him. I took off auto-pilot and got as high as I could. The Spits seeing the danger we were in flew around us to give us some protection...

Later the police found that there were three of them. I am writing about the children. It is time to inject the children into this story. There was the girl, ten years old. There was the older boy, eleven years old. There was the younger boy, ten years old.

> I got on to radio to ground and informed then that I would circle round to use fuel and when I had done so I would bring 'plane in. They were more excited. When I had used up enough fuel I started for ground, as under carriage had

been shot away. I had to sideslip a lot to loose speed. Their air gunners seeing that I could use 'plane had gained some confidence now. The ground staff were excited and I was getting fed up with their chatter. I said for Christ's sake shut up I can manage. I picked out a grassy place and touched down. I didn't do much damage. There was fire and first aid wagons all over the place but I couldn't care less. I had saved crew, 'plane and most important, Myself. I had excitement and being Irish this was part of my life.

I was given decoration. Only the good die young. If any of this I am writing is of any use to you, use it.

I can write about the children with confidence. Much of this is merely notation from official sources anyway.

The children lived a few streets off the park, on the side of the park opposite to the side from which the old man presumably entered. Whenever he could the older boy would get the girl to come into the park after school and there he would cup his hands around her small mounds.

The girl didn't mind too much. But that is conjecture. The older boy thought he ought to like it more. The younger boy would tag along so he could see the older boy cup his hands around the girl's small mounds. These are the children who came into the old man's dying. What have they come out of to do what they did? The old man no longer thinks about things like that.

1 am still trying to trace the ancestry of Man, It's tough going. The fossils are few and far between. In the beginning Man and sub Man. All over the place. The reason that they are all over the place is that once what is

now seas was land. There was once a race of dark skinned people, Not negro. Wandered from Asia to Australia, Some found their way to Tasmania, "What a walk", How they existed in such a place was the survival of the fittest. Then came the white man and trouble, Gin and rum sodden from the hulks and prisons of England, The Tas-Manics shot down or left poisoned meat for the natives whose only crime was that they lived if you would call this living. But had learnt in a hard school and given time would have come to something...

Sixteen days before, after school, the older boy had gone up and whispered something to the girl. She turned her bland blue eyes on him for a moment and then walked away. Later, with the younger boy tagging along, the older boy and the girl met just inside the park's wire strand fence and the three of them walked in. It was wet after the great storm of yesterday, and all the rain overnight. But the older boy was starting to feel his pubescence and they made their way in off the tracks. He was leading the girl and the younger boy. He walked quickly. The girl followed over the wet grass. The younger boy followed them both around the mud areas.. In a clump of trees, the older boy suddenly turned and stood looking at the girl.

She smiled my turn now and

undid her blouse and waited. The bra she had put on to excite the older boy excited the older boy. He came up to her. He cupped his hands around the small mounds and felt himself surge.

It was then that they heard the first scream. It was then that they heard the old man shouting. Not as excited as the older boy or the girl, the younger boy heard it first.

94

It is hard for people such as these people. Any people you like, to adapt to our civilisation and considering things I don't think we have much to offer them. It would be a good idea if all civilisation had a dream time. With the uranium and interfering with genes I don't think it will be long before you have this dream time, "Permanent". The waste from the Uranium is put into drums whose life time is about seven years., "The waste has a life time of about Seven thousand years". Death or malformation is nearer than you think…

The younger boy had heard the old man first. Then the girl. She stiffened even more, still held, as though they were two knobs, by the small mounds by the older boy. The younger boy began to ask *hearit?, hearit?* tremulously. The girl told him ssussh and then the older boy heard it too.

I have chosen to write that the three children heard the old man one at a time. I do so for the dramatic effect. They might have heard it at the same time. Or they might have looked into the storm drain and seen the old man wedged tightly down there and not heard him at all. It does not matter, for the old man was wedged tightly down in the storm drain at that time. Which was his first full day down in the storm drain. Oh, the panicpanicpanic there must have been in him. That is why I have described them hearing him one at a time. It is a way of indicating the old man's drama while describing the children.

Besides I am writing about the early days, *then,* while the old man is writing, as he thinks, from the inner warmth of his council flat in Belfast.

I will now get back to Man and his beginning. I think that what was to be Man started from the chimpanzee who seems to be the most handy regarding the use of hands.

Now comes those Australpithecus, Pithecanthropus, Neanderthal, Cromagnon. I have not made any attempt to put any time for these or other submen or Man, I will give you Professor, J,Z, Young statement of what he considers the ages of Man. Ages xlO^6 years ago. Ramapithecus (14-6), Kenyapithecus, Australopithecus, 3.5, Homo hanilis, Plesianthropus, Robustes (?3.5 — ?0.7), Paranthropus, Zinjanthropus, Homo (?0.5 — recent), H erectus, including Pithecanthropus, Sinanthropus, Zinnjanthropus, Atlanthropus, H erectus erect, (0.5-0.4), H erectus sinecis (0.4-0.25), H sapiens (0.25 —recent) including Javanthropus, Palacoanthropus, Cyphanthropus, Protanthropus, H sapiens steinheimensis (0.25 — 0.20), H sapiens neanderthalesis (0.07-0.045) including solocensis, rhodesiensis, H sapiens sapiens (0.04 —recent).

I thank Professor for this information, J,Z, Young. I hope you have been taking notice.

Together the three children followed the old man's voice to the opening of the storm drain. It was hard to see in,, but not too hard to hear the old man calling for help. They approached the storm drain carefully, especially after the rain of yesterday.

They might not have been conscious that that was the reason they approached the opening cautiously. They might tell you that it was because it was muddy and slippery around the opening to the storm drain. They would probably be right. They never did tell the old man why that or why anything.

During my stay in hospital somewhere my notes on ages of man were mis-laid. I have now found these and ages agree with Prof. Young.

Neanderthal man was destroyed by Cromagnon. There

were four ice ages and those that could not adapt perished. Outside Stockholm harbour there is a statue of Neanderthal Man by Rodin. Neanderthal Man sits there, his legs crossed, Elbow on knee and chin cupped in palm of hand "Thinking", about what? Can't understand how Cro-Magnon had the intelligence to wipe out this thinking race of people.

On his first day down there, as soon as the light had come, the old man had started calling for help. He did it reluctantly at first. He didn't want to cause anybody any trouble. He didn't want to be embarrassed in front of anyone. Back 'home' he had learnt that people hate you if you cause embarrassment or are embarrassed in front of them. (That is an observation that I maintain would explain much of his actions.) He didn't want to cause the trouble of bringing the whole of Sydney down on him.

He started out with a demure, ' Is anyone there?' Let us say that it sounded just as tentative as when he was outside his sister's door asking if there was anybody inside, and her probably hiding behind the door.

Soon the old man began to realise that nobody was coming. That nobody could hear him to make them or him embarrassed about it all. That the world above him, through the opening that made his little old parchment skin crawl, was not alive with rescuers.

So he had started to yell. But it wasn't until he had panicked the first time and screamed that the children heard him. It was a long, muffled way between them and him...

To knock your EGO out of joint you started out as simply a cell, You haven't much to boast about because everything that walks, crawls, otherwise gets about came up from the same thing. I will now start the book on the beginnings of man. What you have read so far has been an Introduction.

On my travels with my family of Mankinde I meet other people like me and yet not so unlike, they are not as hairy as me but seem to be very quarrellsome but they have better tools them I have. I notice their skins are sowen together, not tied. Present day knowledge; This was the meeting between Neanderthal man and Cro-Magnon man, And the disparense of Neanderthal man.

Alas the persuit of knowledge has, it seems ceased and to find an educated man is like trying to find a snowball in hell.

Before he had panicked and got out the scream, the old man had soon become hoarse. He never did have a loud voice anyway. It was more of a piping, so he soon became hoarse trying to call out for help. But mainly, on the first day, he was tired. That is a perfectly good assumption to make. Let us say it had taken him all his strength to keep his little old veiny head above water during the night when the first water rush had come flashing down the storm drain at him.

That first night.
He had had, we are saying, to sit up straining his face upwards, his legs somehow pinned down so that he couldn't move them. The water rush trying to drag his head down. To caress it? That black oily silk. The old man choking on that black oily silk that I have used to describe the storm water in gush in rush in flash. Gagging and squirming while the rubbish thumped against his chest. Soft nudgings in the dark.

This isn't pornographic book, If your mind is full of that kind of filth you are in desperate need of help, A few minutes of pleasure and what then?, sports, Horses, Dogs, TV, Etc Etc, Anything but Education and Thinking. It's a damned good thing we have people who think, If we didn't have these people what a bloody awful world it would be, No classic Music, No washing machines, No 'fridges, No phones, No radio. This is only to mention a few, that makes life comfortable. Do you think? If you don't what a shocking waste of 3 lbs of brain.

Even on the second day, I say that the old man could not see how come his legs could be jammed so. The level of the water in the drain was still too high for him to see his legs. The water in the drain, effluent of the previous night's storm, was too filthy. The little old man could not see through it enough to see how his legs could be wedged in like that.

Did he think of his little council flat back in Belfast and his friends and the silk shirt he had worn coming back 'home' here during those early days? We don't know. It doesn't matter whether he did or not. The way I have shaped this narration about him has him doing all that in the last few days before the last storm's approach. Let's leave it at that, knowing that he might have, would have, must have, wouldn't have, given his ideas on thinking that he is writing to you about...

I am thinking now of SALK, FLEMING, Madame CURIE, to mention a few. Salk is the man who put paid to Polio.

Every endeavour will be made to keep out Scientific terms such as Maths, Cybernetics, Etc, but sometimes I may have to use these to make sense. I would advise you to get Introduction to study of man, J,Z, Young Mechanism of mind, by Edward de Bono. If you don't understand at first try again and again. To gain knowledge you have to try. Knowledge is power.

And the old man was embarrassed because he could not see any logical way his legs could have got stuck so down in there, so at first he only began to call out softly. Now, when he looked up. Now, when he was taking a breather not just because his first scream had made him hoarse but also because it had threatened to shatter his nerves. Now, when he was collecting himself to (not getting used to but) getting used to being down there a bit. Now, about an hour before he vomited for the first time of many times down there during all those days. Now, when he was choking on the stench down there that he would soon get used to. Now, about three hours before the rats began to show themselves.

On the second day. The old man looked up and saw

the children looking down at him.

I hope Professor Young and Edward de Bono will forgive me if I quote from their books, A SUN AN INFERNO OF MATTER, IS THROWN OUT FROM THE GALAXY, PIECES OF THIS WERE SPLIT UP INTO PLANETS ONE OF THESE THE EARTH FIRST STARTED, LIFE AS WE KNOW IT, But the Earth was then in a molten state Rocks, everything was molten, Flames upwards and down again, At last after billions of years things began to

I shall finish that 'began to solidify.'.

The older boy's eyes adjusted to the pitched darkness down in the storm drain first. He couldn't believe his eyes. When the

100

girl and the younger boy could see as well, they, too, couldn't understand at first. What was an old man doing down there?

The old man stared up at them with his cattle eyes. He hadn't heard them coming and, besides, he was still startled by his own first scream. His little old body seeming to flounder trying to catch its breath. So he stared up at them with his cattle eyes. When the girl realised her blouse was open and her bra rucked up above one of her small mounds, she jumped back from the hole of that opening above the old man. (You can see from that which way I am going to go to develop a motive for the children's actions towards the old man. Guilt was their motive as far as the police I spoke to were concerned. It's just as good as any other motive I could think up anyway.)

The older boy and the younger boy jumped back just after her, but only out of getting a fright when she moved so quickly. The old man called out, *'Please...'*

So far all the books I have written you have dealt with men as if women were something second class and inferior, How this came about is something of a misfortune or curse from a bigoted past. This attitude is found mostly in Eastern countries where the women are treated as chattels or something to amuse ones-self with. How much experience I have had in these Eatem countries it will not be necessary to repeat here. I say give the woman the opportunity and she will gain the experience. Without this opportunity she is just something that washes dishes and looks after babies including having them. This is something you can educate and make into something.

The girl was doing up her blouse and blushing. The old man

had seen her with her blouse undone, let us say. He's seen us. He's seen my small mound. He'll *tell*. (I won't pursuit this line unnecessarily.) The older boy knew what she meant by the way she was looking it. The younger boy couldn't understand, but would come to soon. The old man called out, *'Please...'* again. But they did not hear him. They were running away. It was

the last time they would listen to him. But they would come back time and time again... Oh, but he has forgotten all this now — our respective writings (mine and the old man's) have got even farther apart.

There need be no lack of motherhood. Instead you would have something self reliant, If you have a lot of children that is your fault. There are now ways and means to avoid this. Brains is what is wanted and plenty. Send your children to a good school, Books in plenty is required in the home. These combined with brains won't wear out. Get all that jazz together and bum it. If you can't afford the books get to the library. You'll find all the books and help there you require. Now to the woman and the man, If by some misfortune you can't have any children of your own and you are thinking of artificial insemination, Find out all the particulars about his genetics. Was he well educated, a drunkard or just a nothing. If he was either of the last two avoid him like the plague, Remember this child is going to be yours and demand the best "Heredity", The world is hard enough without bestowing a handicap on him or her.

So the old man stayed there down in the storm drain for another two days before the children came back. By that time he had given up calling out. He dare not scream again for his own sake. So he just gave up calling out.

It continued to rain, during the nights mostly.

You (the sun) never shone through down in upon on him much during the days either; in all those days, now that I come to write about it, you never shone through onto the old man, not a living once.

To make sure there is nothing but the best get examined by a pathologist and the man, You will thus be giving your child a flying start. I might seem rather particular to you, Why not?, There are enough ignorant fools in the world. This is your history. Run your eyes up for a moment up the scale of life. At the bottom of life are the Protozoa, the Coelenterates follow in mixed array, the Echinoderms, Worms, Molluscs, Above these come the Piaces, then the Amphibia, then the Reptiles. Then what? Mothers. Then the series stops, Nature has never made anything since. Is it too much to say that the one motive of organic Nature was to make you a Mother. It is the chief thing Nature did, You ask your Zoologist when you next go for your examination. You're turned out by the machinery of Nature designed in the last resort. You will find mothers in every state of imperfection. Old ideas abandonned and new animals coming up to the front. I've already told you all about this. You mustn't get impatient with me. Just use your 3 lbs of brains and think THINK, Thats what you are on earth to do. It is a fact that no human mother can be regarded without reverence. That the goal of the whole universe and animal kingdom has been the creation of a family, which the very naturalist has had Mammalia. In the vegetable kingdom from the Motherlessness of the early Cryptograms, we rise to find a first maternity foreshadowed in the flowering tree. Now may I the writer say something...

And as it happened the sulky weather (of course unusual for this time of the year in Sydney; this is a fictional bubo put on the corpus of a horror reality) kept the number of people you would normally expect to go in the park at this time down to a minimum. An unhearing sparse few, sulkily wrapped up. The old man lay trapped in the heavy centre of a peopleless place. Marooned. Feeling something happening to his legs in that peopleless place...

> Now may I the writer say something again. There is the baby. Helpless, has to be cleaned, fed, warmed. In fact, Everything. All. But what have you got? Everything, If you spend the time he or she can be anything. Now for the training. Get those blasted pill to hell out of it. That little baby has to be taught to speak and gradually put little pieces together, When it first reaches out its hands it has started to think. Don't be impatient, Remember the brain is still growing but it is growing fast and the faster the brain grows the better. It has to be taught to be clean. Little pieces to go together, Harder as it goes along,

When it rained in the early days, the old man let his head lie back and let the rain drops fall onto his upturned little old face. He would also drink as best he could. Purification or something like it. Trying to drink water down there made him throw up as quickly as the stench down there when he thought about the stench down there. He had not eaten for days, he thought.

(He was thinking and was *willing* then. He had not started writing his books to you from the snugness of his snugwarm little Belfast Council flat.)

He was aware that he had not eaten for days. He thought he remembered that he had something in his pocket of his trousers but he could not reach the pocket of his trousers. And when the water had begun to recede, then the mosquitoes had come. All the time the children, too.

In time teach it how to tell the time on the clock, Show some books and teach to read, Don't forget that little brain ticking over all the time, There's quite a lot you can teach it before it goes to school. NOW, whats it to be, Violinist, Scholar, Linguist, Professional or what. That little person depends on you, Astute or a drone. Its in your hands, If one has knowledge it commands respect, Physical powers and beauty are respected but only for a time but knowledge always, Its always easier to play than learn but the rewards are great. Knowledge.

Now to the Mother in you, The tree elaborates the seed or nut or fruit with infinite... No, I won't persue that line of thinking just yet, Your not ready for that yet...

The mosquitoes had come as the water in the storm drain began to recede. The mosquitoes drilled and sucked at the old man as though he was already newly dead. And when the old man tried to move against them he could not seem to want to move against them. They were there, part of the high-pitch whining of the storm drain and of his nerves. Tinnitus, tinnitus. His whole body somehow wedged, just like his little old legs.

And when the water began to recede, he noticed then that the fleas began to hop around in the drying mud banks on either side of the water. I am tempted to add the metaphor of '... like people at the sea-side seen high up' but the old man would not have seen people on a beach from high up, I think. And he could see that, if the water receded much more, his arms would have to lie where the fleas were.

105

He did not like the thought of that and indulged in a self-fulfilling wish that somebody might come before it happened like that.

He indulged in the wish that the children who had come two days ago would return with their mums and dads and people carrying a big strong rope in their arms and maternal sympathy in their hearts.

> In the vagina of a woman there is a thin piece of membrane, This is supposed to denote that she is a virgin, The breakage of this can happen by undue strain but it is not so. In Arabic countries when she has intercourse with her husband the sheet on the following morning is waved outside the window, If the sheet does not show blood the woman is flung out and becomes of no account or a prostitute. This I have seen actually happen, I've been there. Horrible but true. There is now only one place she can go. Sisters street in Alexandria, Egypt. Read this true story and THINK.

The children did come back. I do not need add 'alone'. The three of them looked down at the old man in the storm drain. The girl gasped and the younger boy was wide-eyed. They hadn't believed they had seen what they had seen two days before. Let us say the girl and the older boy were hoping they hadn't. Let us say, too, the girl and the older boy and the younger boy were hoping that they had. Both statements could be true, wholly or partly.

It is now known that the older boy had warned the younger boy not to say anything to anybody. The old man had seen the small mounds of the girl exposed. He could tell why they had gone into the park. They would say that they were nowhere near the storm drain, so how could that old man say things like

106

that about them...? They knew they could whine impressively.

For two days they waited for the accusation. Adults in outrage. But nothing. Nobody had thrashed them. Nobody told of an old man caught down in the storm drain. Nothing and nobody. So they returned to see if they had actually seen an old man down in the storm drain or whether it had been a dream.

I will now write about another woman and her followers. This woman was Mrs Pankhurst about 1906, This woman fought for votes for women, She chained herself to railing and played merry hell with the authorities. She starved and was forced fed and suffered the indigenities the authorities could inflict on her. In spite of all these she won the vote. Now what has happened to the women of Australia? You have the vote, What are you doing about it? You get Politicians in who are not worth a quarter of the money. Who promise everything and do damn all. Theyre going to sell Uranium to everyone, you don't have to be much of a salesman to sell anything to countries who are in desperate need of it. One day this Uranium will be returned to us with devastating effects. The know-how to put this stuff together can be bought...

The old man told them he had come down there to sleep and hadn't woke up until after he had been trapped by the water rush, he thought. They couldn't understand a word he said. They leaned over the opening to the storm drain and strained to listen to the old man speaking to them and raised their eyebrows 'dunno' at each other. The old man thought it must have happened like that.

Already, you see, he was leaving the reality of his 'home' and You not shining down on him much, and removing himself.

107

Soon after this he would be back in his cosy flat in Belfast writing his books to you.

But the old man did speak to them like the little doll they thought he was. He is our own little pet. We found him. They did not say to each other, I surmise, that he could not tell anyone about the girl and the older boy while he stayed trapped down there; they would have just been giggly secretive that they had found their own little living doll. And right out of their own telly wonderland. Finder's keeper.

Have you noticed how a country that is poverty stricken can always find the money for WAR? The world might go out with a BANG. This damned stuff spreads. Van Braum who poured into Briton the buzz bombs and V2 rockets, (Hes now dead, I hope if there is a hell they have found a warmer place than usual for him.) There is a nother thing. Chemical Biological Warfare. This is the last word in frightfulness, 1 will deal with this in another part of my book, With re, the politicians. I don't want a bleat from you I want a roar.

The old man didn't recognise the children when he looked up the second time. Perhaps he had squinted up looking for the great big circling bird to come. Who knows? We can only conjecture. When he saw the children for the second time he began to talk quickly. The children listened to him. They did not move from the edge of the opening above him while they listened to him.

He said for them to go and get help quickly. He said that he was trapped down in this storm drain. He said he didn't know why or how he got trapped down in the storm drain. (He partly lied there, we guess.) He said he thought it was not good for his health to be trapped down in this storm drain where the smell was and where he thought he could hear the shuffling of things down there in the pitch dark and he thought it might be rats and that wasn't nice. He said please go and get someone to help me out. He said, ' I am cold and wet and stuck and hungry and I think I'm aching somewhere'.

Now let's get back to you as a woman. There was a group of women who wanted to determine the sex of their child and how they done it this was described on Channel 2 A,B,C, Sydney. They will no doubt forward you particulars, A woman is equipped with 4000 Ova, These have to last until she is about 45 years of age, I am dealing now with immunology, Now any words I write don't be frightened of them, I will make things as clear as possible, I have no doubt many scholars will be disgusted with me but I could not care less.

A man injects into a woman a million of Sperm. These have to find their way through crevices, fishures etc of the vagina. A lot don't make it but those that do are faced with a swim of 8 inches, Now this swim...

The old man (I write as another layer of embellishment) explained to them that he had got trapped down there by the water rush after the storm. But he could not tell them how come he was down there. We can say now, after the horror that he went through, that he could no longer remember why or how he had arrived down in the storm drain. We can say that because, now, he has to become fictionnonfictionliterature anyway to have his story told, so certain embellishments cannot hurt him. So he did not remember how or why he had arrived down in the storm drain and so he could not tell the children how he had got down there to be trapped by the water rush.

Still, while he could see them hovering at the opening to the storm drain above him, he kept talking at them. They could not hear a word he was saying. But, you see, the thing was (as they say), he

spoke to them in that little piping voice of his like the little living doll that they knew in their hearts of hearts he was. It was the second time that the children had come.

Now this swim is covered with obstacles, One can only enter then the womb closes up and will not allow the passage of any more, (But sometimes two may get in but this is very rare, I will return to this later), Now everything springs into action, Cells are formed. They then split up (Segmentation), Two into four, four into eight, eight into sixteen and so on. These cells form bone, muscles, brains, etc etc. Everything that will make a baby or babies, this one Sperm will make twins, triplets or quads. The mother doesn't like this one bit so she tries to make herself immune against this foreign thing that has been forced upon her so she sets up a barrier against it, The foetus, (Baby) also sets up a barrier against the Mother. The barrier has also to be set up against the Placenta, (after birth). This placenta feeds the foetus and takes away all waste, Everything depends on you, Plenty of milk, Carbon for the foetus, and for you to feed the baby when it arrives.

Now you know the right way to have a baby.

He is our little pet. We can hear the children thinking that when the penny drops that he is in the position of being nothing more than their own little pet with the little thin piping voice they cannot understand. We found him. They did find him. He is our little pet. He certainly became their little pet.

110

They did not say to each other that a little own pet was hardly likely to tell their mas and pas about certain small-mound fiddling after school; it was enough to have a mutual and silent agreement about the novelty of having their own little pet down there in the storm drain 'whaa-whaa'ing up to them. Right out of bizzibuzz bear of telly wonderland. Their own unreal.

Now we come to the trying to have a baby, Your husband seems all right. Are you alright. May be too much acidity in the vagina. Douche with salt water. Still no results, Have withdrawn from your husband some Sperm, Have examined, if O.K. inject into ovum, If still no good, Have examination at hospital, Both. You may be helped by immune suppression. If you have had a fallopian tube tied up you can be helped. I have left a lot out but I have put in the essentials, Now it is up to you to look after yourself, Everything depends on you. I will come to Biology.

He said up to them that he was cold and wet and hungry and caught and it smelt. He asked them to go and get help quickly. He said he was aching somewhere.

He asked them *please.*

This is you X.X. This is the man X.Y. The child when bom if a boy will be X, Y, if a girl X,X. The child that is bom or if it is twins they are both the same, boy's or girl's. If by chance the two Sperms should enter the womb they will not be twins, that is to say they could be a boy and girl, If one should suffer a bum the tissue from one will not graft on to the other. I am now deeding with millions not thousands of millions. The seas were swarming with single celled life, Then came double cells creatures and then three or four cells nobody could count

111

to. Some invaded land and became the first vertebrates.

I hope this makes sense to you, I want THINKERS only, I have made everything as easy as I can without being technical. You will find all in the detailed description I have included.

The little old man told the children that he thought something was wrong with his legs and told them they had to help him because he was Australian; he was 'home'; he was proud of his Irish accent but he was still an adopted Australian so they ought to help one of their own. He told them, as they were listening and not hearing and smiling down at him and not smiling, that if he was back in his little cosysnug council flat in Belfast things would be different, very different. He wouldn't want help; he had all he wanted back in his little council flat in Belfast.

It was on the third day and during the second visit by the children, and already his mind was drifting back to his little wombwalled Belfast flat and the books he had always wanted to write for you.

I shall have to leave this for a time, I have other writings I want to do. I sometimes wonder if I should leave man in his savage state, As I write this I wonder if he has progressed very far. They say any intelligent man shouldn't have an opinion. Well my opinion of man is very poor, Now I'll continue for what it is worth...

Then the children went away. They did not Say anything to one another. They went away from the opening to the storm drain above the old man and they didn't know quite what to think. (I think that is a reasonable assumption to make. They were not *bad* children in the sense of seeping evil.) The old man looked like a little old man down the storm drain. But by the time they had reached the gates to the park they had come to know between them that it was dark down there in the storm drain and they couldn't go too near the edge of the opening to the storm drain because it was slippery and they heard only a smalltinylittle voice saying something up to them just like a pixy or a fairy or, if they had known the word, a leprechaun. Yes, and they knew it had to be a pixy fairy little personthing living doll because if it had been somebody down there like a dirty old man he could snitch on them for the cupping of small mounds. So the children left the park.

That was the second time.

They hadn't said a word to the old man who laid back. The fleas ate at his right arm that night and he stared wide-eyed up through the opening above him. There were no stars, was no moon. But he knew the sky was up there somewhere. The little old man stared upwards wide-eyed. He was full of wonder about possibilities, the possibilities of it all.

From the bee's cell and the butterfly's wing men draw what you call the Argument from what I call the design. Are you reading this closely, I'm not doing this for my own health. I'm doing this so you can THINK, THINK and make your thoughts captive. But it is in the kingdoms which come without observation, in these great immortail orderings which science is but beginning to perceive, that the purpose of Creations is revealed.

Well this is Homo Sapiens and his Ascent. Things as they are point towards his Descent. These I will deal with in later notes,

It will not be beautiful reading but it will be the truth

113

whether you like it or not. Youll get it in book shops.

After school the following day the older boy approached the girl and whispered something in her ear and, with the younger boy tagging along, she met him just inside the park's wire strand fence again. They tracked their wet way back to the storm drain. (It had been raining again the night before, but not enough to send another water rush at the old man, I presume, I assume, I state.) At the opening they edged towards the opening and peered down, holding tight to the earth.

They knew the old man was still down there in his leprechaun place. Pixie, pixie. They could hear him moaning as they slid up to the opening.

The old man grunted when the older boy threw down a small clod of earth on to the old man to make him look up. He was still looking with his mind at that stage. He looked up knowing he was looking up and grunted again when he saw their moon faces moon down upon him down in there. He held up his right hand. Or his left. He held up one of his little old knotty hands and implored them with a gesture with the hand that he was holding up to them.

The younger boy saw that it was all scratched and bleeding, was their own little pixie's hand, but he did not tell the other two. He didn't know that that old man's hand had been scratched and bitten by the rats. And the girl

leaned into the hole and worked her jaw and finally managed to come out with, 'Who are you?'. It came out crossly and anyway the old man had forgotten the children were up there by now; he was returning to his little council flat in Belfast.

I have done quite a lot of studying on this and if at times I make mistakes I am not the only one, I will start from the beginning. I am going to write to you so you can learn all about how YOU came to be you. It might hurt your ego to learn, but I can't help that. It is not for nothing that you are a THINKING human being. For gods sake when are you going to USE IT. Beginning of earth from soler system, 5000. Origin of earth 40000 or formation. Formation of life from inorganic matter or organic, 3955 million. Chemical evelution about 3500 million microfossils?, about 25000 million, Biological evolution. Vegetation had now began to appear, Oxygen had now appeared on earth. I am now dealing with millions not thousands of millions. The seas were swarming with single celled life, Then came double cells creatures, Some invaded land and became the first vertebrates. You will find all this in detailed description I have included. This is the age of the Cambrian rocks. A fossil of a segmented worm found in Australia, Date 650 years. (Millions)

And the younger boy leaned over the opening's edge daringly and asked this old man what he was doing down there. Then the old man began shouting at them. I think we can say, even at this stage, that it was just the old man's voice shouting at them. The old man's voice began shouting at them for all looking down on him in the same way and not telling their mamas and papas and waving his scratched and bleeding hands above him like the two tendrils of an aquarium's seaweed. That is a wrong, a not-apt metaphor to make, but I leave it there to show how wrong and how not-apt it is.

And it had begun to smell down there as well and the girl didn't like it at all and the boys said it wasn't too bad because they had to be boys in front of her. And the three of them waited near the opening to the storm drain, looking at each other, sheltering from the drizzle that had just begun to fall, huddling under the gum tree ten metres away from the opening, and

listening to the raised piping voice of the little old pixie coming out of the hole. Until it petered out.

> The predominant salt within the cells is potassium, Accompanied by small quantities of Sodium, Since the body salts are capable, when dissolved in water of conducting an electric currant, They are called electrolytes, This is all I'm going to tell you about cells.

> As I write this I want to thank all the professors Writers, Musicians etc, who have made life easier for me in my desire for knowledge which even at times if I don't understand I do my best. Sometimes I come up with real gems in this pursuit of wanting to know why. This is by Professor Rosberry: The appearance of life on a place like this is thought to be inevitable, given appropriate conditions, a "Long Success" you might say...

The three children waited a while, perhaps, under the gum by the drain opening until the old man's voice had petered out. Then the older boy crept forward and looked over the edge. When his eyes adjusted again they met the two unblinking eyes of the old man. But quiet now. There but not there. The girl and the younger boy joined the older boy. The older boy hesitated, perhaps, until he was nudged to ask if the old man was hungry. 'Dwant anythingteat?' asked as a child would of a pixie.

The old man's large little unblinking eyes rolled once and he put one fist — let's say the left — into his mouth.

The older boy had a biscuit in his pocket. It was all the

children had. He fished the biscuit that he had out of his pocket and held it up so that the old man's eyes could see.

The old man pleaded for it with his eyes.

The children smiled at one another. Their own little pixie eats. He eats biscuits. The older boy tied a string around the biscuit and lowered it down to the old man. Clever thinking, presuming that the boy did so in order that the biscuit wouldn't fall into the water rather than in order to taunt the old man with it. Well, we have opened up the possibility of either. But the old man did not grab for the biscuit. Instead he grabbed the string and tried, it seems, to heave himself up on it. Frantic for the life-line. And the older boy let the string fall. And the biscuit fell into the slush down there and the old man swooped it up to nibble at it like a little brown starving mouse. Not at all like a pixie really, or perhaps the children weren't so observing. And they were delighted. And they clapped their hands. And they had found what their little own pet wanted. They laughed, in the humorless way children do together to make sure the others know they are laughing too. And this was

on the second occasion that the children had come; it was the third or fourth day. Early days.

That mice could have come out of nothing but com and a dirty shirt in a box in the dark, Maggots could be produced in decaying meat, cockroaches appear without the efforts of the parents in food scraps undisturbed in the kitchen. Our own parasites.

That second time they had come was the first time the children had laughed. The younger boy, when he saw the other two laughing, laughed the loudest, rocking theatrical and trying to impress the other two about how he had the loudest laugh of all time. Not understanding at all why the older boy and the girl were laughing in the first place.

Our own parasites, especially those that are always with you or a part of you, Don't think you haven't got any, You're no different than any other human being since 2500 years (Millions) ago. Our parasites call for the same appraisal of what they are, You're never going to stop trying to get rid of some of them from your body, but there are better reasons for doing things like this than those that spring from prejudice and ignorance. Youve got to keep THINKING.

Now you see what clever men have had to put up with through Bigots, Ignorance and Intolarence.

Around the opening to the storm drain the three children (I write) had worn the grass to mud and the younger boy was still laughing the loudest when he slipped on the mud around the opening. The younger boy wavered off-balanced, tottering over the opening to the dark damp shiveriness of the storm drain down there. Squeaking in alarm. But the older boy, first, and then the girl managed to catch hold of him just in time. Hearts in their mouths for themselves as they did so. They stopped laughing for a while before

the older boy started laughing again. Naughty old pixie.

But from then on they didn't go too near the opening to the storm drain. They never did approach close enough to look down on the old man again. Except once. (And this is my fiction.) From then on the old man was just a sound of a voice or the sound of a voice or, perhaps, a sound of the voice, whichever. Each time they came back to the storm drain, they would creep not right up to the edge of the opening and would

118

listen to hear his voice tones and then would laugh that he should still be there, their own pixie. And with each time they did that, the old man became less real. A voice from the centre of the earth of fairyland. He was a tug of new string and the biscuit magically gone and the small bottle of water empty when they pulled it back up. Everybody knows you should leave good things to eat around for fairies or pixies or Santa Claus. A voice. The voice. Their own unreal.

The descent of Man from the Animal Kingdom is sometimes referred to as a degradation. "It is an unspeakable exultation". Why cant you get that through your heads, THINK how many times do I have to tell you?

I will now try to trace Man's life from the beginning, Where I can't give exact dates I will say 'About'. I have already given you pages about inorganic and organic matter, I suggest you get books on different matters, The Library will give you a great deal of help on this matter. If you read a book from any professor don't take it for granted. Get another book from another professor. I will now come to bits and pieces left in the human body from your distant past.

The three children would sit on the wet grass away from the edge of the opening and nudge each other and giggle don't-tell-him-we're-here and listen to the old man's voice rising unintelligibly up to them from the fairyland depths:

You come into the world like any other animal and you suffer all the diseases that go with it. But you have something that other animals do not have. A Brain. Which could lead to your destruction or immense heights, there is no Decent here but Ascent instead. You have loaded yourself up with religions, Religions beyond count. To believe in these would deny ME, Your CREATOR, No Man can give you absolution from your sins. I have no saints just good men that pointed the way to you, You can pray to me anywhere. I do not need Elaborate Churches or Money, If you commit a sin pray to me for forgiveness. If you are sincere this is granted, But sin no more and help others less fortunate than YOU yourself.

They forgot that the old man's eyes had looked up and seen the girl's small mounds outside her bra. Their own unreal. Once the older boy had a notion to cup the girl's small mounds but she wasn't interested in that anymore. She wanted to get to her own unreal. So did the older boy anyway. Even the younger boy hadn't stopped to watch the older boy move his hands towards the girl's small mounds, but had gone on ahead to sit by the opening.

Their own unreal.

They did not laugh at what the old man was saying. (They did not know he was writing to you back in his womboid little council flat in Belfast, of course.) They could not understand what the old man was saying anyway. All they knew was that it made them laugh and happy and full of adventure.

Forgetting that they had once looked down over the opening and into the pitched darkness (almost) of the storm drain and seen him real. Only the piping little voice at the bottom of their garden. In the storm drain. Disneyland, Disneyland.

Look up into the sky. All this have I made. From inorganic matter I have made you. I have introduced into your earth Prophets who taught you the way. If you have not taken advantage of these Prophets there is no way out.

These are my prophets Mohammed, Isaiah, Jeremiah, Moses, Malachi, Jesus Christ, Confucius, Buddha, Gautama, John the Celt. If you had followed their teaching you would be in a better position when the time comes to meet ME. From an Ape which I have given the power to think and also freedom of choice this choice is yours.

Now I come to the long upward climb, From inorginic matter to orginic matter, The ultimate, Man, Beauty and Beast, More Beast than Beauty. There are of course thousands of other planats in this vast Universe. Stop and look up at the stars, into the sky. You see twinklings points of light, The sophisticated telescopes see much more but there is a lot beyond their reach, Intelligent?, How can we reach them?, not by the speed of light (186,000 per second), Then with what or how?, That is if Man does not blow the Earth out of existence with H bomb, Blow the Earth this way or the other, This way a solid globe of ice, The other way burnt up. Evolution, if it could start again wouldn't stand a chance.

These were in the early days when the little old man's mind was still migrating back and forth between this one place and that one place. Here's the storm drain and the rats and the fleas and the stench and the rain and the no-help and the no-sun and the no great bird and the nobody ever listening and the no food and the no warmth and the no one thing that was Any One Thing at all.

In those early days, I think we can add, the old man occasionally heard whispering and tittering like as if, outside the door of his little snug council flat, children were waiting (could hardly wait) to ambush him. Giggle, giggle. And his little old body would hold still and his little old craggy ear

121

would cock and his mind would stop writing his books to you. And he would listen, ssh, carefully. And then he would know that he could hear the children up there beyond the opening above him. The biscuit and the small Coke bottle of water.

He couldn't remember their faces anymore. His own unreals.

Think back and see what a glorious future lies ahead of you, Think, I want thinkers. Not "Charlatans", Belfast. Killing each other in the name of their god. Black people, Yellow people, All peoples killing each other in the name of god, You get nothing without paying for it and pay you will. I, the writer am not starting a new religion, You have enough, Each one thinking his is better than the other. I will now speak about a great man...

The old man's eyes would watch the grey sky. He would estimate where You (the sun) was. He would guess that if the children were going to come today they would be here soon. The whisperings and the gigglings and the biscuit. In the early days, when he could note that they were there probably, he would almost be glad for the company. When he felt they were all up there sitting around, listening, he would talk to them. Write, you see,

books for them...

May I be forgiven for naming this creature man, I refer to Mussolini who decided to take on the bow and arrow natives of Abyssinia, This was of course to give murderous ruffians the chance to show their skill in new weapons. This creature was later hung in the streets. Now we come to another creature of that ilk, Hitler, who set the world ablaze, all this was of course to right the fancied wrongs of the people. He destroyed by the gas chamber six million jews, the Pope was as usual "silent". It has always been the practice to send out missionarys to soften up the natives for trade or gain, The practice was if you didn't believe in that particular religion was to Bum, Torture, or be-head, In the name of the cross of course, Such as the Spaniards with the inquisition, Again the Popes were silent.

Voices of his whispering, giggling audience and readers in the old man's wandering ear. Dreamtime, lull, lulling lullingly. This was in the early days down in the storm drain, of course. I am still writing about the early days as part of a themic inversion of time you will have recognised long ago. I write too of the possibility that

at these times when the children were there, nudging each other and near to piddling their pants, the old man did not feel alone. He could write his books, sit at his accommodating little desk in his little council flat in Belfast and write his books. But if he did not hear them or they did not come that was the time when his mind would weaken in Sydney down in one of its storm drains and he would weep for the loneliness of it all, for the sunless thing of it all, for the fleas and the rats and the mosquitoes and for the water rush that had somehow wedged him down there and for him hurting somewhere he could not, nor dare not, look.

And for the help that never came.

At those times, his mind locked in the time and place of my narration, the old man would weep. Large wellings out of his little old large brown eyes. But if he thought he could hear the children up there, he did not weep. Instead he lullingly dreamt on lulled...

Henrey the VIII made religion suit him, Now we come to the great and mighty U.S.A. with their slavery, Can anything be said in favour of this brutality, The slaves were taught about Jesus Christ, I wonder what the slaves thought about the mercy of Jesus in their misery, Now the slavers are in slavery themselves, They are afraid of Advanced Technology. People are beginning to think, No longer is the white man supreme. Through out thousand millions of years have peoples suffered from gods, priests, ministers when above and around them was the CREATOR of this vast universe.

Now this is the last day that the children came. The second rat (remember?) sits on the debris that pins the old man's legs in the slush. The last storm is approaching.

Only there is the last pause now. (Remember?)

The world is hushed. The old man, having scared the rats away for the last time (but they have only retreated a little way, watching the second rat move on down closer; remember?) lies back in his exhausted little old rotting body and is still now to our reading eyes. The part of his mind that is still, only just, peeking shyly through into a consciousness of time (Sydney) and place (the storm drain) does not know how far away the last water rush is. It does not care much, I assume. It hopes it might be soon, perhaps even I can assume. It is only in this last pause of the last storm at this moment.

The way has been hard but always upward. Inspite of all that has happened and will happen rest assured that there is a brighter future for you, To those that suffer, Your suffering has not been in vain. I the writer have also suffered and am still suffering. I have served in two world wars, R,N,A,S, — R,A,F. France, Egypt. The suffering I

124

have seen is beyond imagination, France, Spotting from kite balloon behind the lines for artillaiy, Shot down twice, Bailed out, Powers in charge decided to send us to Egypt, Was brought back, Tunic and all clothing taken off and steamed, The rest of us thrown in creosote tank to get rid of lice, Was put on train, Floors covered, carriages were there for horses and smelt like it, Through France and Italy, Stops for food and drink and toilet use. Sailed to Port Said, Escorted by Japan Navy, Egypt shocked me, poverty, Flies, Mosquitoes, Sand all the time, Frozen at night, burnt up through the day, When it rained as it did once a year it never stopped, I was 18 years of age then.

This is the last day the children come. They stand shushing each other by the gum near the opening of the storm drain. They prepare to sneak up to near the opening and listen to see if they can hear their own little pixie still there to make them giggle. They have been caught in the last shower of rain that cascaded down on to the old man's face. The children are wet now. They will have to explain how they got as wet and muddy as they are going to get soon. Today the girl hadn't wanted to come. There is a storm coming up, she said. But the older boy is feeling his pubescence growing heavier on him day by day and coaxed her into the park. The younger boy stood back and respectfully watched him cup her small mounds in his hands again. But his mind, like the minds of the older boy and the girl in fact, was more on the opening of the storm drain below where their own pixie might be again this day.

Now, at last, they creep squelchingly near to the opening.

1939, 1 was in London then, British asked for men who had been in previous war to give their services again, 'Planes this time, France and Egypt again. I made a great mistake when I joined up again, I put my war ribbons on so naturally everyone turned to me as a man of experience, Instead of marching in fours everyone was marching in threes. I had to learn, quickly, so back to books, Whilst others were out enjoying themselves I was intent on books on movements, guns etc. Books are friends. They teach you how to think quickly, how to be astute and if you get into trouble how to get out of it with lightening speed, you are alert and out think the other fellow.

Since the last time they had come, the coughing had started. The old man's body has started coughing, but he does not know he is. The coughs make his little old upper body shake like a chain. The girl hears this. The older boy hears this. The younger boy hears it. They hear the coughing that is nothing that their own unreal should do. The girl crawls forward, careful not to slip in the mud around the opening. The boys crawl forward carefully, following her. The girl and the two boys look over the edge of the opening. Carefully. Squinting their eyes up against the darkness down in there. The light is poor everywhere. The last storm is approaching.

Soon the water rush.

Now it is the last pause, breathless, hushlessful. The children peering fearfully down into the hole where the coughing comes from. The smell is overpowering them. The two boys turn their heads aside, but the girl braces herself to keep peering down. It is enough for the girl's eyes to adjust to the light. She sees

the old man's eyes looking up at her. Unblinking and motionless in their frames.

She catches sight of a movement. The girl forces her eyes away from the old man's little large brown motionless eyes and focuses on the movement.

She sees around the old man's legs, rats. Rats. Boiling around the old man's legs. The rats. They have come now. The girl sees the rats in swamp swarm at the old man's legs. She screams. The boys scream with her, out of fright. They run. The children run. They dash through the eye of the coming last storm towards telling their mamas and papas that there is a real old man trapped down the storm drain. Not their own unreal after all.

The little old man lies motionless.

> Now we will come to the question of skill. Parents, if you think anything of that boy or girl make sure that he or she has skill and if you can afford it send him or her to a first class school, But when school is over for the day you are not finished, there is home work to be done. When I was very young I attended Christian Brothers College, A Brother called Sweeny taught me and one of the things he insisted on was " I'll teach you a lesson, but i don't want it repeated like a parrot, I want you to think the lesson out and repeat it in your own original idea." This is where Edward de Bono conies in...

It was found
that the three children had been visiting the old man on and off for sixteen days. Biscuits and water apart, the children had visited on and off for sixteen days with their whisperings and their gigglings. And finding a new piece of string each day. For most of the last of those days they had visited the court held in the council flats in Belfast.

If your mind is clouded up this will get you straight, I want you to have your children taught Music, When I say Music I mean just that, I don't mean this so- called Music, Jazz, This is easily learnt and anything that is easily learnt isn't worth bothering about. Get a violin, leam all about the notes. Get a teacher, go into a room that isn't used much, close the door, put a mute on the bridge of violin and go to it. It won't be easy but anything that's worth doing isn't easy. The repayments are great. Knowledge is "Power". I am living in a Salvation Hostel,

(I don't think he is, but this is the confusion of our joint writings; I think it is in a comforting little council flat in Belfast),

I have room to myself, A clean bed and as much food as I need. I don't bother them much and they don't bother me, I have nothing but praise for them although I think that they think I am a bit queer...

It was found
that the children had heard the old man talking to them. He might have asked them to go for help, but they could not understand him. No, it was found, they didn't actually see the old man. They had not dared to go too near the opening to the storm drain, they said. Neither the girl nor the older boy nor the younger boy could talk about the rats at swamp swarm at the old man's legs. They did not have to agree between themselves not to mention that.

I can or you can dig a hole in the ground but once the hole is there you without skill are finished, but I as a plumber, as I once was take over, I hope you get my meaning. Regarding my religion I believe in a Creator, indeed I would find it hard to disbelieve. Watch that violinist, his

128

hands fly over the strings, To be able to do this has meant hours and hours of hard work. He has Hands, Two marvellous instruments, There is nothing on earth like these hands, But they are of no use without a brain, This you have even if you haven't used it. There is plenty of space in this brain for anyone who is prepared to use it. Without a knowledge of Books, Music etc, you are uneducated. I am surrounded by books and what I don't have I get from the Library thanks to them. They have been very good to me, You go along and try.

Now I am back writing about the last pause on the last day surrounding the old man. This is the here-and-now of this story if you like; but more importantly, it is the here-and- now of the last storm. The old man might have heard the girl first and then the two boys scream when she saw the rats. It matters nothing if I speculate whether he did or not, so I will do both. The thoughts of the children the rats the lizard, perhaps even the great bird up there where You haven't shone through very much all the time he has been 'home'... all these, I write, have now passed out of the old man's mind, however much they were or were not in his mind to start with. Only

his little particle of here-and-now consciousness still peeks out of-his eye's mind waiting for the water rush, like a thrilling friend, to come.

Let me return to Egypt, Alexandria. At one time the Turks drove all the females they didn't want out, They found their ways to Alexandria and set up the only business they knew. Prostitutes. This was in Sisters St, Off rue de la Marine, This is one of the horrors of war. There were others in Cairo, but one took a risk here, they were not licensed and were examined by a doctor. I have in my travels believed in making friends with what you would name the common people, I refer to one young egyptian (Hamedo) who took me into places where an ordinary British person would take his life into his hands, The Lingo he taught me, I could then go by my self without any trouble.

The old man does not feel anymore. The rats don't bother him anymore. The fleas the mosquitoes the rain the cold the aching the wet, they do not bother him much anymore. He is passing the time with his books and his writings waiting for You to shine down on him a little bit more. And we have also said that there is just a small part of him that is waiting for the last storm and the last water rush to come.

I have travelled all over Briton, Scotland, Wales, Ireland and the Isle of Man, when younger rode Norton in T.T. Broke a shoulder blade, That put paid to that. I have found majority of Australians illitrate. They have Gods, The king of them all is Money, The worship of this God is beyond belief, They have other God's, these are Football, cricket, horses, The better class of books are not in the race, You are respected if you have the first God, It's not what you know that counts, it is how much you have. I have worked (as a plumber) in better class houses. Good books, Unopened, "For show".

Almost at the last, we can say this: The old man suddenly has a feeling that he is being transported out of his snug little warm council cosy flat in Belfast and is finding himself at an airport. He has on the white silk shirt that he hasn't worn since he left Australia to come back home (not the irenic, ironic quotation marks there) here to Belfast all those tens of years ago. He is distinctly feeling all of a sudden that he is wearing this white shirt at this airport and there are people seeing him off. But then

130

he suddenly feels they are not seeing him off but meeting him. They are pointing at his little silk white shirt he bought all those years ago and meeting him as he steps off an aeroplane. And he suddenly is feeling that there should be people waiting to greet him as he steps off the aeroplane but there is only a voice and a sisterly form behind the door hiding. He feels, suddenly, in this vision,

alone. Landed. His own unreal to himself. He feels

there are three tiny little voices whispering and giggling around him and those voices are saying that he is in Sydney and in a dark place, in a hole of a place. They are tormenting him with being way back in Sydney after all these years and lonely and wet and cold and *dying* (yes!) in a hole of a place. What more will they torment him with?

Now I write that, in panic, the old man's mind frantically casts around itself and finds that it is still safe and lodged sound in the little council flat that is his own in Belfast. His very own real.

You enter a hotel and talk about anything else but the above Gods you are treated as something QUEER, if you ask for the radio to be turned on to some decent Music you are strange. I am an Irishman from a long, long way back, I confess I don't understand your politics but you have all got what you have asked for. I haven't seen politicians get a, country in such a state in such a short time. You will no doubt ask what the hell I am doing here, Well I was a first class plumber and sheet metal worker and you advertised for people like me, on the boat I went there were Carpenters, Painters, Bricklayers, plumbers etc. Each man had test for trade, education, Physical.

Meanwhile
the older boy is running well ahead of the other two children.

The older boy has reached the road before the girl and the younger boy.

Meanwhile
it begins to rain the last of the rains.

I will now come to the great U,S,A, Having bled England nearly stone dead she decided to come into the war, England invented the H, BOMB only the U,S,A, had the money to make it.

There are a good many so called writers use words like (fuck) (shit), These to my way of thinking should be written as intercourse, Excreta. Perhaps this is to bloody clean for you. When I am that way inclined I will write you a filthy book, But as regards Filth I have my limits.

Now I will come to another subject; A Primate, I had not as yet a very high degree of intelligence. I was just another hairy creature with no fangs or claws, I live on berries and small animals but can make traps to catch larger animals, I was generationing a small brain and enough intelligence to keep out of danger, CLEVER, I had by now the use of fire I started by lightning, I could frighten other animals or hunt with burning limbs of trees.

I have now found out the way to make fire, This I used to drive bears and other large animals out of caves, These animals being in a state of hibernation, SLEEPY, With sharp pieces of flint and stone I skinned these animals and outer skins as covering for me. The caves I used for living in.

132

Meanwhile
the older boy has stopped a man who was hurrying past
because the last of the rains has already started. The older boy
tries to tell the man that there is an old man trapped down the
storm drain over in there and the girl and the younger boy
have joined him. But the man is getting wet and tells the
children to go home and tell their parents about whatever's
worrying them. That's what parents are for. It is starting to
rain hard. The man has brushed past them making for some
shelter.

Meanwhile
the light in the folds of the last storm is going so fast that the
old man's unblinking little old large brown eyes cannot see the
sky anymore. If he was looking.

Instead of playing with bits of stone formed thousands of
millions of years ago we play with Helium, Disease
structured to suit the enemy who seeks to destroy
whatever the suffering and suffering you will have. But in
this coming war everyone will suffer. It will be complete
annihilation of this planet. This planet had failures but it
also had beauty.

Meanwhile
the children run on. It is starting to hurt now, running in the
hail that is starting to hurt now. Going towards home with a
story that is starting to hurt now.

The U.S. has gone completely mad, They invent new
weapons and taunt the U.S.S.R. and create ill-will where
it shouldn't exist. From one state of frightfulness to
another. A certain Von Braum who was the inventor of
the Buzz Bomb and rocket who bombed the hell out of
Britain was captured by U.S. who made full use of his

133

intelligence (if you could call it that), I have been in two world wars so I know what all the frightfulness is all about. Look up and around you, Could man make anything like this.

Meanwhile
the children now have swung into the home of the older boy and have stopped suddenly under the shelter of the porch there as the hail hisses and the rain beats its way against the wind and the air becomes latently brown. Outside there, around the old man and the children, both. Meanwhile the children have second thoughts about how they can tell about the old man. Meanwhile the old man appears to be listening to the final passage of the last storm and could almost be said to be appearing to nod yesyes.

Religions. There are thousands of these, the majority of them will promise you easy ways to heven, My religion is a CREATOR of this whole vast universe. It is easy and costs nothing. If you can't do any good, do no evil, Help those less able. If you are suffering your beauty is yet to come. You can pray to your CREATOR any time, any place. Death does not exist. Comfort one another,

The End.

To professors: Try and agree.

I must insert this if I have not already done so. Immunology. The Germans used the skin of jews to cover parts of A.O.R. crews burnt up in crashes. But so that the skin wouldn't be rejected the skin had to be rendered immune.

Meanwhile

the older boy's father has come out of the house and onto the porch, cross with his son. The children would not have told even then had the girl been able to hold back her sobs from breaking into crocodile tears at the sight of the older boy's father and had the eyes of the boys not been so red-rimmed.

As I come to close this book I find my head a jungle of ideas formed and ill-formed. From a few wisps of nebulous matter we have come to this. From a long range of evolution we have come to this. From a savage to a savage, but a sophisticated savage.

It is recorded that
the father of the older boy threw the coat he had hanging in the hallway over his shoulders and ran through the hail-stones to the comer shop. There the father of the older boy used the telephone. He called the only police number that he knew, the emergency one. It was a TV emergency one he remembered. It was the right one amazingly.

I shall go on with thoughts that don't bear thinking about. I had just the average amount of brains. I was not prepared to go to any thinking that would help me make a name for myself. I met this fellow through having a fight with him about religion, name of Ozzie. As I think back, what a stupid thing to be fighting about. Any way we became friends after that. I was envious of him. I became his very firm friend although I was still envious of him. But I knew I couldn't compete with him. I consider after what I have learnt I was bloody lucky to get out of this fight without a severe beating.

It is recorded that
particulars concerning an alleged old man trapped in a central park storm drain for an alleged number of days were taken

down over the telephone. It is recorded that the caller alleged he was the father of a boy who had allegedly come across the old man whilst playing in the park. It is recorded that this seemed to be a genuine call and recommended to be treated as an emergency.

This Ozzie started to learn the Violin. It amazed me how quickly he learnt, I was apprentice plumber as he was and as usual he out-classed me. It wasn't long before he started off playing in dance halls at first but in a short time he was playing solos in the intervals in the cinemas. He was still practising all hours and working as well, He must have had a wonderful vitality. He picked up a girl in a dance hall. I am not surprised at this. The girls used to throw themselves at him. This girl was a beauty. He introduced me to her. She had a beautiful face and figure, Sparkling, intelligent eyes. She didn't seem to walk but slide, "Beauty at its best", I suppose her dancing would account for this. I thought to myself, you bastard you get everything, but this wasn't fair he worked hard at everything he done. He used to keep a taxi waiting whilst playing in cinemas and when he had finished playing his solo he would go off to another cinema and play another solo. I went to the cinema to listen...

It is recorded that
the local police station was contacted from central control almost immediately that the fire brigade was also alerted that the local constable drove immediately around to the address that central control had given to him that the alleged father had given to it;

that
there, that constable spoke to three children and that he did not need much time to be convinced they weren't lying and that

136

the parents of the girl and the parents of the younger boy had now gathered at that same address and that the constable and two of the fathers took the older boy out of the house and that they hurried off into the park with the older boy.

... to listen to him and there is no doubt about it he was great. You could have heard a pin drop while he was playing and the audience went mad for more. He now left the cinemas and went into leading orchestras as leading violinist. In evening clothes this Ozzie was a handsome bastard and I am not surprised women fell for him. He played Paganini Concertano at the town hall and got letters after his name. He couldn't do a damned thing wrong.

It is recorded that
when the party arrived at the storm drain they could see nothing at first. They had to be careful because without the cover over the opening it was dangerous and muddy there.

I am not finished with this fellow yet. His carrying onwith women was a disgrace but I couldn't blame him very much for this considering the way women used to go out of their way to meet him. He had a violin and he used to treat it like a baby and God help anyone who tried to look down on him. He couldn't care less about Dukes, Earls or whatever the hell you were. If you talked and he was playing he would tell you to "Shut Up" with a few curses thrown in. But still for all of that he was generous, i,e, If you couldn't afford to pay his fees he would teach for nothing. But woe betide you if he had given you a lesson to learn and you made the same mistake. He could curse like a trooper...

It is recorded that

the opening to the storm drain lay off to one side and the party could see nothing at first because it was all seething water right down in there and it stank to high heaven down in there and. Besides, the last water rush had come spewing down the storm drain. Spewed up by the last rains of the last storm.

Now I will come to his wife. She was left in the background while all this was going on and they separated. This is only what I heard. She had a baby to him and so-called friends told her about stuff to take that would get rid of the baby, this killed her, she got Brights disease and it killed her, he went to visit her "once" in hospital, she was in terrible pain and baby died. This one visit to hospital was the last time she seen him, I hope his conscience is bothering him now. If it hadn't been for these other women I believe they could have made a go of it. He lost a truly delicious creature. I wish she had belonged to me, In my opinion none of the others came within a mile of her. I think the violin and intelligence ruined him.

It was also recorded that
when they descended the ladder to get the old man out they still did not believe there was an old man down there to get out. When they descended the ladder to get the alleged old man out, the stench was such that they thought there might be leaking gas somewhere. It was recorded that the constable and one of the fathers (I would only be presuming if I ventured which father in this, my fiction) threw up until they were retching dry where they found the old man. It doesn't matter now.

Ozzie had plenty of courage though as evidenced by his exploits in France and Middle East, They thought that much of him that they offered him a commission which

138

he refused. I don't know whether I would do this kind of stuff he did or not...

(This is Edward Nugent writing this).

... I don't know whether I would carry on like this or not but I probably would. I think this would be to my shame. I am not going to write a war book, Theres enough of these to start another war. I have already written about the futilities of war, I have seen beauty but I have seen a hell of a lot of misery. More misery than beauty caused by war. People seem to be at their worst in wars. The "victors"

It was also recorded that
they eventually had to use three crowbars to lift the debris that had pinned the old man's legs in the mud. It is also recorded that they all moved back involuntarily when they finally got the debris lifted that was pinning the little old man's legs down in that mud down in there. The old man did not look like a man anymore, so they said. It was recorded that they had to wait three days before bothering to get his body (I have avoided the use of the term 'remains' here, but I do not know why) out. After the last storm it had taken three days for the water from the water rush to begin to recede. Three days even.

Thoughts. This will be the start of my new book. I want you thinkers, not dead as DODOS...

(My first novel was called DOGOD. DODOS, his spelling; DOGOD, my spelling. Now I too am becoming confused.)

... Where are you? I am not writing this for nothing you know. I shall start off by saying that if you don't find the commas and full stops in the right place and some words not as they should be I couldn't care less.

I will come to the Salvation Army. I have the utmost admiration for these people. They give you clean bed, As much food as you can eat and plenty of hot water and leave you alone, The water, Once I was glad to get water I could drink. I have a clean small flat, Own small T,v, Plenty of cassettes, Classic Music, Plenty of Literature, In fact everything that an educated person would want or need.

I will now come to the Aborigines. These people with a very distant past did not invite you to come here, No, You came with guns, rum, whips and a very brutish past, The scum of British jails and a lot of religions which you preached but did not carry out, How could you expect these coloured people with a religion superior to yours to understand you. You took their country from them and tried to civilise them, Wow, What a word "Civilise", Preach Jesus Christ and take a man out and whip him to death.

Now, confusedly, I am going back in time to when the last storm for the old man is mounting. This is the death of all pastels. That is my observation of the colour of the world around the death of the old man. I *associate,* perhaps and certainly unnecessarily. I write, too: You are shut out in final joust. Not even I know what I mean by that. But there is a foreboding in the very grouping of the words that make me want to leave them in here. I do so. I confess that, when I think about it, the 'You' I mean to be You (the sun). It therefore links up with a sentence before which read: This is the death of all pastels. I repeatrewrite: You are shut out in final joust.

For the last storm is mounting on the old man now.

What is left of the old man here in this storm drain in this Sydney nods to itself/himself without nodding. The old man braces himself without bracing himself. The old man watches and waits for the water rush now without watching and waiting. Now. Now, and is thinking of the writing and the thinking.

Is it any wonder that Aborigines couldn't understand you and still don't. To them it doesn't, Make sense. I will now come to the white Australians, In war, Bravery, Yes, Fighting qualities, Yes, Savages, Yes, Cario for instance, Drunken australians, They put nearly all Cario out of bounds. They don't want the past brought up, No wonder. Read History of australia, The original Aussies are barred from certain places, Does this mean that you consider that you are superior to them?, How long do you think you'd live under the conditions they lived?, You have wall to wall carpets, first class houses, good food, everything in fact that makes life worth living, I'd wonder who'd last the longest, I wonder whether I should call you uneducated or ill-educated, Books, you have plenty, What kind?, Music you have plenty, what kind? We see these hairy creatures get up and strum on their instruments and what issues from their mouth is supposed to be singing, This is called by some people "Talent". All your best Artists get to hell out of it, eg Joan Sutherland and many others, Still you have left that one great which you all worship "MONEY", The more ostentatious you are the better you are or so you believe. Greeks, Italians, etc, etc, to whom we owe so much culture are named as Dagos, Wogs etc. You take a good look at yourself, get THINKING.

YOU ARE THE SUN. A SUN AN INFERNO OF MATTER IS THROWN OUT FROM THE GALAXY, PIECES OF THIS SUN WERE SPLIT UP INTO PLANETS, ONE OF THESE THE EARTH FIRST STARTED, LIFE AS WE KNOW IT, But the Earth was then in a molten state Rocks,

Everything was molten, Flames upwards and downwards all over the shop, At last after billions of years things began to solidityfy.

Are the minds, morals of men to be warped, judged, by the machines or atom for the purpose of war?

They will be judged, all men are one no matter what colour or greed. Poetry felt, but never knew that the universe was one. The sciences link us to the stars, That surely is enough to make you THINK, Use your brain, I thank professors and the like for this information I give to YOU.

The heading of this book I will call THOUGHTS, It is what everything is what everything is about, You see something, A thought is started but you haven't got the time to do anything about it now. The thought was started, Thought is master of thinking so when you have the time you will start thinking about what you have noted.

I once had this happen to me. The word Kamsa, kept coming into my mind, It had no realionship with what I was doing, I shoved it back into my brain for further processing. Several days afterwards it came back to me that it meant 5 in Arabic, why this should come up I don't know as it had no connection with what I was doing.

Now I will come to that parasite of the human brain, (however beautifill it is) THE BODY. Clothes to keep it warm, take the clothes off to keep it cool, if you don't excrete, Laxitives required here if not normal, urinate, in fact it seems endless the things this body needs and wants. All this so that brain shall have a good supply of blood.

Without a very active brain, life would seem like hell to me if such a place like hell exists, I appreciate flowers, the perfume, beauty and beautifill music.

Now
here in this storm drain in Sydney
once and for all
the here-and-now of the storm drain of Sydney of the last storm of the coming water rush must have registered with the old man: that

now
here once and for all the water rush to come soon. The last storm, the final storm, has broken. The final sky burst. He knows it is seething outside.

The storm water pouring in looping swirls along all the gutters. Swerving into all the gutters, seeking the drain. It seeks the drains. It seeks the storm drain. It seeks the old man. It floods for the underground openings. It drains for the underground floodings. It spouts and pours, it runs, it cascades. The old man's eyes blink for the first time in register of the here-and-now.

The old man's eyes are seeing now.

They still look upwards through the water blurr. But now they blink. The old man is seeing now. Even the rain pouring down

143

through the opening to the storm drain above him is hurting now. He blinks in register of the here- and-now:

> I am an Irishman so I don't give a damn what you call me. My ancestry stretches back a long long way. You'll no doubt think why don't I get out of the country. Well you wanted first class tradesmen so I came. I have been in two wars and being an Irish man I wasn't compelled to join any wars. Join the Library, Think, That is very necessary, To Think. This won't please any one, I couldn't care less, Av waa, This is French for I'll see you later. It isn't spelt this way. You have some educated people but they are few and far between.

> I am now living in an intellectual desert. I am now living in an intellectual desert.

> I am now living in an intellectual desert.

He knows now, does the old man, that there will be no more You (the sun). He feels the air current suck back into the drain way down there somewhere. I write that he hears the air current being sucked away down in there away in the drain somewhere. He tastes the wet air, I write, being sucked so strongly into the drain that it makes him feel so light he might just go with it.

And feeling, hearing, seeing, tasting, smelling, knowing (I write), *acquiring* by every sense of his now sense of the here-and-now (I write) the growing rumble mounting somewhere down there in the storm drain. The growing water rush. The mounting water rush. The

water rush seminally in surge somewhere further down in the storm drain.

144

It comes. It comes. The old man does not tense himself. It comes. He cannot tense himself. That is over now. The water rush. It has come. Now.

On the beach. On the beach before I left to come out here, I wrote my name in the sand three times, In three rows about two yards high each row, Found a stick washed up by the sea, eg Man when evolution started, Picked it up and wrote my name in the sand there with it, I thought, If I'm going I'm going to leave my name behind...

But there is too much weight upon the old man's legs. The water rush doesn't shift the weight from off the old man's legs. His legs remain held fast — this is what must have happened; it is not my fancy; here I am not confused — and his little old torso floats freely in the water rush now. The old man's face is still uplifted, but he cannot see through the inkysilken water up to the opening above him there now. He cannot wait for You (the sun) any longer. His upper body floats within the body of the water now.

The old man's body floats gently there and back now.

Three times, each time about two yards high, My name, I wrote it with a stick I found washed up by the sea I suppose, If I'm going I'm going to leave my name behind, I wrote it in big capitol letters, I wrote my name all sorts of ways, even copperplate, Characters in Dickins wrote in copperplate in case you didn't know, Get your local Librarian to help you. I thought I'd leave my mark. Then this great big wave came in, "The largest wave they had ever seen", This great wave came in and woosh! Thats all the thanks you get. Woosh! Washed it all away. Woosh!, Washed it all away. Woosh!, Washed it all away. Woosh! Washed it all away. Woosh! Washed it all away. Woosh!

Washed it all away. Woosh! Wa

(Edward Nugent adds to the final book proofs:
'The old man has gone devoutly to his Creator'.)

----0000----